THE SECRET PACT

The Battle Ends, the War Continues
in Secret

GLEN CARTY

Acknowledgements

My sincerest thanks to:

Acacia Cunningham for her careful proofreading; should any
errors remain, they are entirely mine
The cast of Beta readers for their valuable feedback
My wife for her enduring support

In the remote mountains of a lush, vibrant land, where the sun cast its golden rays upon the sprawling fields and dense forests, there existed two villages—several miles apart yet connected by traditions and tribal ceremonies. Among these villages lived two young souls, destined to intertwine their fates in a way neither could foresee.

THE RAINBOW

K ai, a young Maroon boy, was in high spirits as he set out on the familiar path. He lived in a village called Crawford Town, on the banks of the Spanish River. It was his birthday, and his favorite time of year, when the air held a crispness that invigorated his spirit. He was now fifteen years old, no longer a child but not quite a man, caught in that space where youthful energy grappled with the weight of experience and the measure of balance.

For two-thirds of his life, the harsh realities of conflict had shaped his existence, defining his very sense of self. The transition from a life consumed by war to one of peace was not an instantaneous shift but a gradual process of relearning and rediscovery. With the arrival of peace, Kai found himself navigating uncharted territory, learning to reconcile his warrior's instincts with the quiet demands of ordinary life.

Hunting became a refuge for Kai, a way to channel the warrior spirit that still burned within him. In the silent depths of the forest, he found solace in the rhythmic pulse of his own heartbeat. The crackle of dry leaves, once evoking fear and caution as the footsteps of unseen enemies, transformed into a familiar and comforting sound. Now, it symbolized the natural rhythm of the forest—a mongoose darting through the underbrush, or a bird taking flight from its perch. Each rustle of leaves, each snap of a twig, served as a reminder of nature's resilience and the enduring spirit of the land.

His footsteps were sure and steady as he navigated the winding trails, his senses keen to the sights and sounds of the forest around him. His destination lay ahead, a place he called his sanctuary among his favorite trees, the Flame of the Forest. As Kai reached the crest of the hill, the view of the expansive Blue Mountain range always took his breath away. To the south, a vast expanse of lush greenery stretched before him, the vibrant hues of the forest painting a picture of untamed beauty. On a nearby mountain slope, another large copse of his favorite tree was in full bloom, their canopies so dense with orange-scarlet flowers that the hill appeared to be ablaze.

His father told him it was a sacred tree. A reminder of their ancestral home of Africa where it was known as the African Tulip, a majestic tree reaching heights of 60ft or more. He said in much the same way the tree never lost its splendor and majesty, even after being transplanted over a thousand miles to a foreign land, so too could the Maroon people rise up and achieve greatness. The stories of the Flame of the Forest always stirred something deep within Kai, filling him with a sense of connection to his roots and heritage.

But the majestic tree held more than just symbolic value for Kai and his village. His friends had their own playful nickname for the tree—Donkey Pee Pee—a name derived from the liquid that oozed from its banana-shaped flower buds. The children delighted in playing with the swollen buds, their laughter echoing as they took turns giving them a good squeeze, sending the watery nectar squirting as far as ten feet.

Yet, beyond the amusement of the children, the tree held profound healing properties. The local medicine lady knew its secrets well, using the liquid from the pods as eye drops to treat various ailments. With careful precision, she would squeeze several drops of the precious liquid directly into her patient's eye, harnessing the natural power of the Flame of the Forest to bring relief and comfort. Other parts of the tree were used to treat a variety of ailments, from colds to stomach aches, showcasing the deep connection between the Maroon people and the natural world that surrounded them.

To the east of where he sat was Nanny Town, another Maroon village. It was also called New Nanny Town because the original village of the same name had been invaded and occupied by the British. The village was empty when the British arrived; the Maroons had vanished like ghosts. The new town was much higher in the mountains than Kai's village. Mountains so high that their peaks were often hidden in the clouds. Many miles separated the villages, a distance so great that the mountains appeared blue in the distance. The two villages would on occasion get together for special ceremonies, but beyond that, contact between them was infrequent.

The rift between the two villages had finally begun to heal. They were united by a shared history of struggle and triumph, but distrust had torn them apart. After the war, the two village leaders had been at odds. Kai's village had signed the British agreement, seeking peace, but Nanny Town had refused, not liking the terms. Nanny, their leader, was angry at Quao, the leader of Kai's village, for signing without her agreement. This extended the war for a few more months before Nanny signed. The rift caused by their disagreement had strained the relationship between the two villages for years. It was only in the past eighteen months or so that progress had been made in repairing the strained relations between the villages—a fragile peace built on mutual respect and a shared desire for unity.

It was during a tribal ceremony to celebrate unity and ancestral rituals in Nanny Town, that Kai first laid eyes on her. She moved with grace, she wore a beautiful Gele, a headwrap of her ancestral heritage. She danced to the rhythmic beats of drums, her eyes a deep, captivating shade of brown that seemed to hold a thousand untold stories. Her name was Willow, the daughter of Nanny, the village leader, and her presence exuded an ethereal aura that drew Kai's gaze like a moth to flame.

Their meeting was fleeting and their words few and hesitant, but an inexplicable connection formed between them —a silent understanding that transcended the boundaries of their respective villages. As the ceremony drew to a close, Kai found himself captivated by the memory of her, the girl whose eyes held a secret world waiting to be discovered.

The rest of the ceremony passed in a daze. Kai's mind was

filled with visions of Willow's warm gaze. He left that night with a burning desire to see her again, his thoughts consumed by the possibility of their paths crossing once more.

. . .

Days turned into weeks, yet he couldn't shake the memory of Willow. His daily routines—hunting, training, long walks—felt hollow, lacking the spark she had ignited in him. He missed her smile, the way her eyes held unspoken understanding, things he hadn't realized he needed until they met.

His walks grew longer, each step unconsciously leading him closer to her village. One afternoon, while exploring a hidden valley, he stumbled upon a waterfall, its veil of shimmering water catching the sunlight. As he marveled at its beauty, a voice drifted toward him—clear, sweet, and filled with a wistful melody. Hidden behind a curtain of vines, he saw Willow, her clothes damp from doing laundry in the river.

For a moment, he froze. It was her, the girl from the ceremony. Should he hide, or...? Hope and nerves tangled inside him, pushing him forward.

He stepped into view. Willow startled, her song cut short. She looked at him, eyes widening in surprise, but quickly softened into a smile as she recognized him. It was the mysterious boy who had held her gaze for so long the night of the ancestral ceremony. She had felt a connection that night, and in fact, found herself thinking about him just moments before he appeared. Surprise mingled with a flicker of gladness.

An awkward silence fell, but then he pointed at a Flame of the Forest tree on the far bank, and told of the funny name they had for it. She laughed, a joyous sound that made something in him relax. Turns out her village had the same name for the flower.

"My mother," Kai said, "before she died, used to say they were torches lit by the warrior spirits to guide our men home from battle." He hesitated, momentarily lost in her memories.

Willow sensing the subtle change, gently probed. "I'm so sorry, the war was hard on all of us... How did she die?"

"She was sick. I'll tell you about it sometime." Kai responded, snapping back to the moment.

Willow studied his face for a moment, a flicker of empathy

in her eyes. "I understand," she replied softly. After a small hesitation, she added, "But that means we'll need to meet again, for me to hear your story." Her smile was sly but encouraging, her eyes a hint of playful mischief.

It was the start of something—they talked for a couple of hours, their initial shyness dissolving with each shared story. They spoke of their lives, their dreams, stories passed down from their elders.

"Look," Willow breathed, her voice barely a whisper. She pointed upwards, her finger trembling slightly.

Kai followed her gaze; a delicate rainbow arched across the sky, hanging in the mists of the falls, in front of the trees and the blue sky. "I've never seen one so close," he murmured in awe.

"My grandmother always said the rainbow is our ancestors smiling down on us," Willow whispered. "A sign of approval."

Her words touched him, bringing back the memories of his mother. "Yes. I think they're pleased..., my mother with them." he murmured. Their eyes met, a warmth kindled within them, a silent understanding was forged under that ephemeral sign.

They agreed to meet again, and with each meeting, their bond deepened, their affection blossoming into something more profound than words could express.

But their stolen moments weren't as secret as they thought. A hidden threat was taking shape. Taro, a young Maroon from Willow's village harboring his own feelings for her, grew increasingly curious about her frequent disappearances. He had long nursed a secret crush on her, admiring the quiet way she listened and the fire in her eyes when she spoke of their people's history. Moreover, being the daughter of Nanny, the well-known warrior, only added to her allure. Taro noticed a change in her, especially upon her return from her walks. She seemed to walk with a lighter step, a newfound warmth in her smile.

His curiosity slowly turned into suspicion. Where did she vanish to, so often? His curiosity, then suspicion, became an obsession. One fateful day, fueled by this need to know, he followed her, keeping to the shadows as she slipped away from the village. His footsteps led him to a clearing amongst some trees, the ground littered with the fallen orange-red flowers.

The sight that unfolded before him—Willow and Kai, lost in their own world—was a knife to his heart. The warmth of their connection was palpable, a silent language that spoke of a bond far deeper than any he could ever imagine for himself.

Jealousy, fury, and betrayal clawed at Taro. Their love felt stolen, a possession he believed was rightfully his. Consumed by rage, a plan ignited in his mind. He would twist his knowledge of the mountains, their hidden pathways and forgotten lore, into a weapon. Their secret rendezvous would be exposed, leaving Kai isolated and ostracized. The villagers would see him as an outsider, a threat to their traditions.

2

CRACKS IN THE FACADE

Taro nursed a seething envy towards Kai, whose natural abilities and prowess seemed to eclipse his own efforts. Taro's father, a renowned warrior and one of Nanny's esteemed captains, commanded immense respect within the village. As his son, Taro inherited a portion of that admiration, and he reveled in the shared prestige.

Taro's self-worth and confidence were deeply intertwined with his father's legacy. Growing up in the shadow of Jeddo's renowned status, Taro's identity was shaped by the admiration and respect his father commanded. He didn't just inherit his father's name; he inherited a sense of purpose and belonging that came with being Jeddo's son. As a result, Taro's own sense of worthiness was closely tied to the image of his father.

All that changed when tragedy struck and Jeddo met his untimely demise in an unprovoked attack by a startled wild boar. He was unarmed, and the animal tore into him, leaving him mortally wounded, plunging the village into a state of disbelief and despair. His death wasn't quick, it was a slow painful one, and as Taro watched the vitality and life drain from his bedridden father, Taro's world began to crumble. His own sense of worthiness died with his father. Suddenly, the adoration of his peers and his association with Nanny seemed hollow, leaving Taro adrift in a sea of uncertainty and insecurity.

As Taro struggled to come to terms with his loss, his long-standing crush on Willow took a turn. He still had a crush, but he no longer felt like he measured up, and the self-confidence he once felt turned to jealousy of anyone who got close to Willow. He struggled for balance—his world had always revolved around his father.

When Taro witnessed Willow's growing closeness to Kai, a newcomer from another village, his jealousy reached a boiling point. Kai's effortless charm and the attention he received from Willow only served to amplify Taro's feelings of inadequacy and resentment. Determined to reclaim what he had lost and win Willow's affection, Taro plotted to befriend Kai, seeing in him both a rival and a means to achieve his own ends.

Approaching Kai with a practiced smile, Taro knew that winning his trust was paramount to his plan. Engaging him in conversation, Taro feigned interest in Kai's hunting skills and mountain lore, masking his true intentions behind a veneer of camaraderie. To Taro's surprise, Kai responded warmly, unaware of the jealousy festering within his supposed friend.

As days turned into weeks, Taro orchestrated opportunities to deepen his bond with Kai. He offered his assistance in any way possible, eagerly joining him on training expeditions and lending a helping hand whenever needed. When Taro extended an invitation for Kai to join an upcoming boar hunt, ostensibly to avenge Taro's father's death, Kai readily accepted. He believed himself to be valued and trusted by his newfound friend, unaware of the ulterior motives lurking beneath Taro's friendly facade.

But behind Taro's affable facade lay a darker purpose. He knew the dangers of the hunt, and he wagered on Kai's downfall to secure his own ascent. Whether by injury, or by the hand of the very beast they sought, Taro saw in the hunt the perfect opportunity to rid himself of his rival once and for all, and perhaps win Willow's favor in the process.

The day before the hunt, Willow and Kai met in their favorite spot: a glade under the flame of the forest tree. As they hugged, Kai mentioned he missed her yesterday and asked if everything was alright.

Willow hesitated, her gaze flickering away for a moment before meeting Kai's concerned eyes. "I'm sorry about that," she replied, her tone soft but tinged with something elusive. "My mother needed my help, and it was too late when we were done."

Kai searched her face, sensing there was more beneath her words. "Are you sure everything's okay? You seem... troubled."

"I'm fine," she said, smiling, but her eyes betrayed a hint of unease. "I'm just worried about you," she admitted, her voice barely above a whisper. "With the hunt approaching and... everything that happened to Jeddo, I can't help but feel anxious."

The evening was chilly as they snuggled for warmth at the base of the tree. "I'll be fine," he replied, though both were thinking about the upcoming hunt.

"Are you nervous?" she asked softly.

Kai shook his head, but a flicker of concern played across his eyes. "A little," he admitted, "but more excited. It's a chance to prove myself. It's the first time that I'll be hunting without my father."

Willow placed a hand on his arm, her touch grounding him. "Maybe that's why I'm uneasy. I know you are strong and not rash. You are a thinker." she said, her voice filled with conviction. "Don't change that because you're out with Taro and the others. You have nothing to prove. Boars are dangerous creatures, especially this one. He killed Taro's father."

Kai squeezed her hand reassuringly. "I'll be careful, I promise. I'll return to you by nightfall, with stories of my bravery," he said, smiling playfully.

They fell into a comfortable silence, each alone with their thoughts but content to be in each other's presence. The sounds of the forest surrounded them—the rustling of leaves, the chirping of the crickets, and tree frogs. Yet, all Kai could hear was the gentle beat of Willow's heart against his chest, a rhythm that mirrored the quiet confidence he carried within himself.

Willow silently whispered a prayer for his safe return. His presence gave her a sense of safety, yet guilt gnawed at her conscience. She had planned to tell him, but the timing was wrong. It was the first time she had lied to him, and it tore her up. Should she burden him before his hunt, with the real reason why she missed their meeting? Or stay silent and wait until his safe return? Each option felt worse than the other, twisting her insides like a wrung cloth. She knew she couldn't keep it a secret forever; her actions placed them all in great peril. Perhaps it was best to wait till he returned.

.   .   .

On the day of the hunt, the air crackled with anticipation. The four young maroon men, their faces painted with the green and brown of the undergrowth, crept through the dense foliage, their senses attuned to the faintest rustle of leaves and the distant snort of a boar. They had been tracking the beast for hours, their hearts pounding with a mixture of fear and exhilaration.

Kai, held his spear tight, its polished tip glinting in the dappled sunlight that filtered through the canopy. Taro was carrying the spear he inherited from his father. As they ventured deeper into the jungle, the air grew thick and humid. The boar's scent, heavy and musky, hung in the air, guiding them towards a steep ravine hidden behind a tangle of vines. Taro signaled to his companions, Jiro, Kenji, and Kai, and they formed a tight circle around the ravine's edge.

Below, they saw it. The boar, a massive beast with thick hide and razor-sharp tusks, was trapped in a narrow crevice. Its eyes, red and wild, darted around as it tried to find an escape route. The boys' hearts hammered in their chests, a primal fear battling with the thrill of the hunt.

Kai knew this was their chance. He glanced at his companions, each face a mask of determination. With a silent nod, they began their descent, their movements slow and deliberate. The boar, sensing their presence, let out a guttural roar that echoed through the ravine. The boys quickened their pace, adrenaline coursing through their veins.

Suddenly, the ground beneath Kenji's feet gave way. He let out a scream as he plunged down the ravine, landing hard on the rocks below. The other boys froze, their eyes wide with horror. Kai reacted first, throwing himself down the slope after his fellow hunter.

He found Kenji lying motionless at the bottom of the ravine, his leg twisted at an unnatural angle. A bone protruded from his skin, stark and white against the green moss. Kai knew instantly that the leg was broken.

Panic threatened to engulf him, but Kai forced himself to stay calm. He knew he had to act quickly. He ripped off a strip of his shirt and fashioned a splint for Kenji's leg, using vines to secure it.

With Kenji secured, Kai turned his attention to the boar. The beast was enraged, its eyes filled with bloodlust. Kai knew he had to kill it before it could harm Kenji or any of them.

With a deep breath, Kai charged towards the boar. He dodged a swipe of its tusks and plunged his spear into the beast's shoulder. The boar roared in pain, but it was not enough to stop it. It charged again, knocking Kai to the ground.

He lay there, stunned, as the boar loomed over him. He closed his eyes, bracing for the final blow, and tensing for the deep piercing of the animal's tusk. But it never came. He heard a cry, a thud, and then silence.

He opened his eyes to see Jiro standing over him, his spear dripping with blood. The boar lay dead at his feet. Relief washed over Kai, followed by a wave of gratitude for his friend.

Taro had not moved, he was riveted with fear and too stunned to move. Realizing the boar was dead, he seized the opportunity to turn a venomous gaze towards Kai. With feigned concern, he accused Kai of reckless hunting, claiming his carelessness caused the injury. His words, laced with malice and deceit, resonated through the shocked silence of the remaining hunters.

Kenji, broke the silence, "No he didn't," he shouted. "I slipped on some loose rocks and I fell. I would have been killed had it not been for Kai."

"I agree," piped in Jiro.

"You are both wrong," shouted Taro. "You could have all been killed. I saw it all. Kai got scared and backed into Kenji, causing him to slip. Then he tried to run away and slipped. I had a line on the boar, but every time I went to throw my spear, Kai would get in the way, putting us all at risk."

Kai was stunned, he could not believe what he was hearing. He was bewildered at Taro's accusation and the venomous tone he used to accuse him. Kenji and Jiro both remained silent.

Taro and Jiro were the first to arrive in the village, carrying the heavy boar between them. Kai arrived much later, assisting the injured Kenji who could hardly walk. It was a slow, arduous walk back. By the time they arrived, Taro's accusations, though baseless, had already spread like wildfire through the village. Kai, caught in the web of Taro's lies, found himself ostracized and shunned. Whispers turned into accusations, and soon, the village elders were demanding an explanation.

Heartbroken and bewildered, Kai stood before the council, his voice trembling as he defended himself. But the seed of doubt, planted by Taro's poisonous words, had already taken root. His words fell on deaf ears, drowned out by the rising tide of suspicion and disapproval. Jiro, fearing Taro's wrath, refused to take sides. He said he was distracted and only saw the boar charge, so he leapt and plunged his spear into the beast. Kenji, who was laid up in bed, also chose to avoid any challenge to Taro's story. They knew Taro well, he was one to hold a grudge, and it was better to not cross him.

As the sun dipped below a far mountain, casting long shadows across the village, Kai stood alone, his heart heavy with despair. The love that had once bloomed in secret now threatened to wither under the harsh judgment of their community. But despite all this, a flicker of hope remained. Willow, despite the fear and pressure she faced, stood unwavering in her support. Their bond, forged in the crucible of hardship, promised to be their only shield against the treacherous tides of deceit.

3

THE WARRIOR QUEEN

The flames crackled and danced in the center of Nanny's hut, casting flickering shadows on the intricately woven tapestries that adorned the walls. Taro sat opposite the tribal leader, herself a great warrior, who had known the boy's father, Jeddo, for most of her life.

"Long ago," she began, her voice carrying the weight of years gone by, "there was a time when our lands faced a grave threat from the English, one that threatened our very existence. Our people, scattered across this island, were united and fought as one. But, the English were cunning, they offered a treaty to sow seeds of discord. Our Brothers in the west accepted the treaty, agreeing to peace and at the same time fracturing the unity we had forged. But our people, here in the Blue Mountains, remained steadfast in our resolve. We fought on, willing to die rather than lose the life we knew."

Taro watched her intently, hanging on every word.

"Taro," she said, "our strength lies in our unity. If you bind ten pieces of thread, it becomes much stronger. It takes but a single tug to break a single thread, but the ten, together, require the force of one hundred tugs to break. The English knew this, so they sought to divide us, and it worked. They offered Quao, the leader of our Crawford Town Brothers—someone I trusted —a treaty to end the war, and he accepted it."

Nanny paused as she relived the memory. Taro, intently

staring at her, waiting for her to continue.

"I was angry with Quao. We were not consulted, yet we were expected to abide by the terms. I saw it as a betrayal to every Maroon in these mountains, so for many months we refused to give up. We chose to continue our resistance and for months, we fought, your father, my most trusted Captain, at my side. In the end, we relented and agreed to the treaty. The war left scars upon our lands and our hearts, brothers betraying brothers, families torn apart. But the worst of it was the damage to the unity and trust that we shared with our brothers in Crawford Town."

"But, you didn't have to give up!" cried Taro. "I was outside the hut, the night the council discussed the treaty. I heard my father say to the council that we should continue to fight. Many agreed."

"You are correct, Taro," she said. "We all left that meeting with a resolve to continue our fight. Too much was at stake. We had been betrayed twice—first by Cudjoe, then by Quao—for terms much worse than the terms given to Cudjoe."

The boy was surprised to hear her agree with him. "Then why did we agree to peace," he asked.

The silence pierced the room, as Nanny searched for the right words to communicate what happened that night. The fire crackled against the backdrop of chirping crickets and frogs. A Patoo, hooted from outside Nanny's hut. As if a signal, she continued...

"I've always had 'The Gift', from a child. In our most dire moments, our Ancestors would visit me..."

.   .   .

That night, I was summoned to Two Claws Peak, the top of a mountain about six miles away. I don't know why that specific summit was chosen; there are others much closer. It was late April, the air was misty and cold. I felt the weight of our future upon my shoulders. I didn't know exactly where I was going, but a Patoo kept flying ahead. It would fly a distance, then perch, then fly again when I came close. I realized it was sent to guide my path, so I followed it. The path was difficult, with areas where the trail was no more than fifteen inches wide, hugging the mountain to one side, steep gorges on the other. One slip meant certain death, but the bird never left my sight.

The mist kept growing thicker with each step as I approached the summit. Then, amidst the swirling fog, I saw the spirits of my ancestors—figures whose bodies were the mist itself. Their faces bore the marks of past and present struggles, and of our future triumphs.

"You've walked a great distance to get here," spoke an elder spirit, in a voice resonating with the wisdom of time. "Your fight with the British is noble, but the road ahead is uncertain, not unlike the path you've been on. The bird we sent is a reminder we are always watching over you."

I stood among these spectral beings with reverence and determination.

"You've led our people bravely, but ahead lies a path fraught with challenges."

"I cannot waver," I replied firmly. "The future of our existence is at risk, our brothers have taken a different path, leaving us divided and weakened. We must fight or be subjugated."

A sage-like figure stepped forward, draped in wispy garb, the texture of the mist and the color of a green budding shoot. "Unity has been our strength, Nanny. But true strength lies in knowing when to wield diplomacy as a weapon."

"Are you saying we should surrender and agree to a truce?" I asked, uncertainty clouding my thoughts.

"Not a surrender, but a strategic move," a spectral warrior asserted. "To secure a peace that grants us space to fortify our people, to gather strength for the trials ahead."

I pondered their words, feeling the weight of their advice settling upon me. "But how can we trust those who have enslaved and oppressed us?"

"The treaty isn't a concession of our freedom," a spectral matriarch assured. "It's a temporary accord, a ceasefire to consolidate our power, to safeguard our traditions, and ensure the survival of our people."

Their voices resonated through the mountains, urging me to see beyond the immediate struggle.

"Let us forge a treaty, not from weakness, but from strategy," advised an ancestral warrior. "To secure our foothold, protect our heritage, and ensure our people endure."

I was suddenly struck by the realization that wars are not won with one battle. Victory is the culmination of wins, losses and concessions. Their wisdom, distilled through generations of resilience, guided my decision. I understood then—it wasn't surrender; it was a calculated step towards securing our future.

With a solemn nod, I accepted the counsel of my ancestors. Their guidance was clear. I would sign the treaty, not in submission, but as a strategic move—a respite to fortify my people for the enduring struggle ahead.

. . .

Taro watched in awe as she began her tale, being pulled in with every word spoken. He was transfixed by what he saw. It appeared her body was in the room, but her consciousness was elsewhere, in another realm. As she concluded the story, her expression shifted from one of distant storytelling to a more grounded awareness. She blinked a few times, taking in the face of the boy, gradually reorienting herself to the physical space and with a soft sigh, she shook her head gently, as if to dispel any lingering traces of the trance that had momentarily consumed her.

"The next day," she said in a calm, soft voice, "I called a meeting of the Council and told them what our Ancestors said. We all saw the wisdom of their words, and we all agreed to accept the Treaty."

The boy listened intently, processing what he had heard.

"Trust once squandered is hard to regain," she continued. "It took us many years to rebuild the trust that was broken between our people. But eventually, over the course of many years, we put aside our differences and worked tirelessly to rebuild the trust that had been shattered."

Nanny paused in deep thought, weighing the gravity of the situation. She looked at Taro, for a duration that felt like an eternity to the boy, and a stare that felt like it pierced his soul. Then she said; "Now, the choice that you make has the potential to put that all at risk."

"True strength," Nanny said, her voice filled with unwavering conviction, "lies not in power, but in the courage to do what is right, even when it is difficult. Choose the path of honor, Taro, and claim the legacy your father so rightfully earned."

4

DAY OF JUDGEMENT

"**I** can't understand why he would lie," Kai said. "I thought he was my friend."

They were sitting in the hut, where Kai was instructed to remain while the elders of the Council deliberated.

Kai's shoulders slumped, the weight of the lie pulling him down like a stone tied to his waist. Willow's light touch on his arm was a fleeting comfort against the chilling grip of Taro's betrayal. "Maami," she said in a steady, reassuring manner, "she sees past the ripples."

Confusion tugged at Kai's brow. "What do you mean?"

Willow met his gaze, and for a minute, he saw Nanny's steely resolve in her eyes. "She has an uncanny way of sensing when something is not the way it seems. She calls it her second sight. It guided her through the war, helping her to avoid many enemy traps."

A spark of hope flickered in Kai's chest. "What do you think will happen?" he asked.

"I don't know," Willow replied. "She knows who you are. I've told her about us. She knows you wouldn't lie about this."

Kai was taken aback by her words, "She... she knows about us?" he stammered, "What did she say?"

He knew it was inevitable. Nanny had to be told how they felt for each other, but he was dreading her reaction. He was intimidated by her achievement. She, a revered fighter and a

17

cunning strategist, known across the island. He was from another village, an outsider, and wasn't sure if he would measure up to her standards.

Seeing his bewilderment, Willow cupped his cheek, and looked in his eyes. "I know you feared her judgment," she murmured. "Maami is a warrior, but her heart beats not just for battles won, but for stories yet to be told. She understands love, and she wants the best for me."

He saw then, not the daughter of a warrior, but a warrior herself, not wielding a blade, but a shield of hope forged in the fire of their love.

"She believes... in me?" he breathed, the question a fragile hope.

"Shhh...," Willow whispered, "She believes in us, and that..., is our best hope."

Willow was conflicted as she said the words. How could she offer comfort when she herself was guilty of a crime far greater. A crime she committed of free will, knowing fully the consequences. One that could mean the loss of her freedom or her life, and one that could destroy both villages. She wanted to tell him, but wouldn't that be selfish? Telling him would make him complicit, also putting his freedom or his life at risk.

. . .

The morning mist hugged the ground around the hut, the air thick with the scent of wet earth. The walls of woven strips of bamboo, encased in mud, showed evidence of years of wear. Sections of mud had crumbled, leaving bare the woven bamboo skeleton. Exploited by the rising sun, sunlight peeked through the exposed bamboo slats, covering Kai's back with dappled light.

The faint, warbling echo of a rooster's crow in the distance was echoed seconds later by another, much closer, that seemed to erupt from somewhere just outside. Kai was jolted from a deep sleep. Willow had left shortly after their talk, but he could not sleep. He had been up most of the night, his thoughts preoccupied with the day's events and what news the next would bring. He had only slept a couple of hours before he was awoken by the rooster.

There was rustling outside the hut, then Willow walked through the door. He sensed something was wrong. She seemed perturbed.

"What's wrong?" he asked.

"I was sent to get you. The council will be meeting soon."

"Have they decided?"

"I don't know. Hurry up." she insisted.

The Council was already seated, and the room was half full with villagers when they arrived. Taro and Nanny had not yet arrived.

Kai was instructed to sit before the Council, to their left. Willow took a standing position not far behind him but, at an angle where he could see her. She wanted him to know he was not alone in this. The room was filled with low whispers as the room got more crowded. Kai could feel their piercing eyes boring holes into his soul, trying to unearth the truth.

The room went silent as Nanny and Taro entered. Taro was directed to sit to the right of the Council as Nanny strode confidently to the front of the room. With her back to the other elders of the Council, their stoic faces reflecting the gravity of the situation, she addressed the room in a firm, loud voice.

"A great wrong has been done. It is our duty, under the watchful gaze of our ancestors, and bound under our ancient oath, to uphold justice and truth. We must find truth and enforce justice.

I spent the evening with Taro, son of Jeddo, my most trusted captain, reminding him of who we are, and the heavy price that was paid, to get us where we are. He has had the night to think about our talk and the legacy of his father, earned through his bravery and integrity."

She paused, shifting her gaze away from her audience to Taro's face, who was looking down.

"It is a legacy that is his to take, if he chooses. All it takes is to live by its values."

He looked up at that moment and their eyes locked, neither backing down. The room was pregnant with silence, the stare feeling like minutes, though a mere few seconds. Taro looked down, breaking the trance, choosing to avert her scrutiny that felt like a probe of his innermost being.

"Do you have anything to say," she asked, "before we begin?"

The room was silent, all attention focused on Taro, with

occasional glances of curiosity towards Kai to gauge his reaction. Kai felt as though he stood on the edge of a cliff, teetering forward moments before gravity's cold embrace would pull him into a plunge to his death. All it would take was a warm, reaching hand to grab the scruff of his neck and pull him back to safety. Taro's next actions held that power. What he did next could either be the cold hands sealing his fate or the warm ones pulling him back from the edge of certain destruction.

After a long pregnant pause, Taro stood up, facing Nanny and the Council, he bowed his head and said:

"I am the son of Jeddo and I have always wanted to be like him. Nanny told me that true strength lies not in power, but in the courage to do what is right, even when it is difficult. Those words have echoed in my head all night."

The room was silent, wondering what he would say. He continued:

"I have stumbled, bringing dishonor to the name of my father. I know the path to regaining your trust is long. I accept any punishment you see fit and I promise you, I will rise from the ashes of this deceit and be the man I wish to become."

Turning to Kai, he said. "Kai, I cannot undo the harm I've caused, but I can offer you this apology; bitter as it may be. Forgive me, if you can, for I have only my own guilt and remorse to offer as penance."

His voice trailed off, leaving a heavy silence in its wake. He had confessed, stripped himself bare, and now he stood before them, vulnerable and raw, waiting for the storm of judgment to break.

Kai felt a mix of relief, elation, and exhaustion, but the weight of exhaustion was most pronounced. The warm hands of Taro's confession had saved him. With that, he was free, and his reputation was restored. Glancing into the audience, he spotted Jiro and Kenji standing at the back of the crowd, behind him. Kenji leaned on crutches, and they had clearly chosen their location to stay out of Kai's immediate line of sight. Relief was written on their faces as they looked at Kai, mirroring the relief he felt. Yet, there was also regret in their eyes—for not being stronger, for not defending him, for not telling the truth. Kai understood their predicament and silently voiced reassurance: 'It's okay. It's over now.' He saw their relief as they both silently mouthed back, "I'm sorry."

Nanny turned towards the other elders of the council, as they gathered in a huddle. A few minutes later, she turned and faced Taro, waiting for the noisy room to settle, then she announced the verdict.

"Taro, your actions have not only wounded Kai but severed the trust that binds this village. Worse yet, your action placed at risk the trust between our villages that took years to rebuild. You must understand the gravity of your transgression."

She paused, her gaze searching Taro's eyes for understanding before continuing. "Your confession took courage and must be recognized. To admit fault, when you have so much to lose, shows integrity. However, integrity alone cannot mend the fractures caused by betrayal."

Nanny's voice softened as she outlined Taro's punishment. "Your penance will be a labor of redemption, a journey to the Blue Mountain Peak through the backcountry, by way of Old Nanny Town. There, where our ancestors rest, you will spend one night, honoring their memory and seeking their guidance. Then, under the watchful gaze of our forebears, you will ascend to the Mountain Peak."

Nanny's gaze drifted toward the window, where the distant peaks of the Blue Mountain Range loomed against the blue sky. "For six nights," she spoke, her voice carrying the weight of her words, "you will dwell within the view of the land for which so many across this country gave their lives, amidst the echoes of our ancestors' sacrifices and the whispers of our sacred homeland.

With a sweeping gesture, she encompassed the significance of the view outside. "Use this time to reflect, to seek your destiny, and to find your true self," she concluded, her eyes returning to rest on Taro.

She then turned to Kai, and said, "You have been wrongfully accused, and for this, we apologize. You have handled yourself with dignity. You never once lashed out in anger, showing restraint, integrity, and respect. You are free to leave, and we humbly beg that you forgive us all that we have wronged you."

Turning to the audience, she said, "This matter is closed and we have a lot to be thankful for. Truth prevails. It took courage to confess, let's afford Taro the respect he deserves for doing the right thing, and not speak of this anymore." She looked over at Jiro and Kenji, "Jiro," she said, "let's share in a feast of that pig."

"Yes, Mam," he said grinning, with a hobbling Kenji at his side, grinning from ear to ear. Kenji knew he could have been killed by the boar, had Kai not intervened. He vowed, he would be a friend, no matter the cost or the risk.

Willow stopped Kai as he began to leave, "Don't leave yet, Maami wants to meet you."

He immediately felt nervous, the weight of her legendary status settling heavily on his shoulders. Feelings of inadequacy rushing back, knowing that she knew about their relationship. Willow sensed his unease and whispered words of encouragement.

He studied Nanny as she walked over. Her ebony skin, etched with raised scars; written tales of countless battles and hard-won victories. She greeted him with a warmth that surprised him. "You're the one my daughter speaks so highly of," she said, her voice a blend of reassurance and authority.

Kai swallowed hard, feeling the intensity of Nanny's gaze upon him. "Yes, ma'am," he replied, his voice surprisingly confident, belying what he felt earlier. "She speaks highly of you too. I've heard many stories of your bravery, and your leadership. I don't know what to say."

Nanny held his gaze, her eyes piercing through his words, seeking the truth hidden in the soul. She saw the reflection of her own spirit, the burning ember of liberty, the unwavering will to sacrifice for what he loved. Her eyes softened as a slow smile spread across her face.

She extended a hand towards him. "A warrior's strength is not merely measured by battles won or legends forged. It resides in the heart, in the love and respect for those around you. If my daughter sees something in you, then I trust her judgment. Your actions today and during the hunt spoke louder than any introduction could. You have the heart of a warrior."

He reached out, accepting her hand in a firm handshake. A sense of acceptance washed over him, a silent acknowledgment passing between them."

Willow was elated as she thanked her mother. She knew her mother's acceptance was the reassurance Kai needed. "Thank you, Maami." she said, smiling.

Nanny smiled back. "Now come," as she turned to the door, "both of you follow me."

She led them to a clearing bathed in the morning sun. Pointing to a single, luminescent spiderweb clinging to a branch, she spoke.

"See this web, spun with delicate thread? It seems fragile, yet it's strong enough to resist the wind, or the touch of clumsy fingers. But," she paused, her gaze heavy with meaning, "even the strongest web can be snagged, torn by a careless brush, a hidden thorn."

She took Willow's hand and placed in it a smooth stone, its surface cool against her palm. "Hold this, Willow. Let it be a reminder to tread carefully, to listen with your heart as well as your ears. And you, Kai," she turned to him, her eyes holding the wisdom of generations, "let your strength be a shield, not a sword. Protect Willow, but do not blind her to the dangers that lie ahead."

She said no more, with that, she turned and walked her way.

Willow felt panic rising. She had seen this before, her mother must have had a dream, or an omen of some sort. Maami sensed her secret and she wanted to warn them.

She turned to Kai with resolve, "Come," she said with authority, "we must talk." Then she turned and headed to the waterfalls where they first met.

5

WILLOW'S SECRET

They sat at her favorite spot at the base of the falls, beside a huge rock by the bank of the river. From there she had a full view of the cascading falls. If she was lucky, there would be a rainbow, her regard for them was more than beauty, but whispers of her ancestors, their smiles carried on the mist. To her, the pools below, churned by the waterfall's fury, mirrored her soul, sifting and swirling, filtering through an unending deluge of thoughts. The ones worth keeping, sinking to its depths, a place of stillness and unruffled calm, while those she must let go, joined the river's flow.

A big boulder, gnarly and ancient, was lodged in the middle of the river directly across from her perch, rising directly in front of the falls. The direction of the currents was slit by its presence, forcing them to choose a path before rejoining on the far side. Its size was almost unimaginable, its broad back supporting gnarled trees that clung tenaciously to its crevices. Thick roots, like the veins of a weathered hand, snaked down its sides, a testament to its resilience against the relentless assault of the water. Sometimes when conflicted about a choice, she would let the river decide. She would focus on the path of an object caught in the currents. Her decision would hinge on its choice. Would it go left or right of the boulder, carried by the current's whims? And if it made it through to the far side surviving the rocky gauntlet, it would be a further sign, a confirmation of timing.

He sensed her struggle within her. Was it Nanny's words or was it something deeper? He knew to wait, to give her the space she needed.

She descended to the water's edge, returning with a smooth stone and a leaf. With a whispered prayer, she wrapped the leaf around the stone, her brow furrowed in concentration. Then, with a flick of her wrist, she sent it sailing into the roiling chaos of the falls.

She rejoined him, her eyes riveted to the leaf, a frail green boat tossed on the torrent. It swirled in the chaos of the pool, submerging only to reemerge moments later in calmer waters flowing downstream. The large boulder stood in its way, forcing the water to flow around it. The leaf spun, caught in eddies, being pushed and pulled, a captive of indecision. Then, a sudden surge, a flicker of resolve, and it broke free, committing to the path towards them. Hope flared in her eyes.

She watched it go by, only to be snagged by a small pool, trapped amongst stones and rocks. Hope dimmed to anxiety as it danced in the pool, finally settling against a rock. Hope faded, then settled into a dull ache as the leaf spun in its watery prison. Frustration etched lines on her face, followed by confusion, a slow acceptance settling over her. Just then an errant current washed into the pool, raising the leaf over the shallow wall of stones. Unconsciously, she took a deep breath, the spark of hope returning to her eyes. The butterfly wasn't dead, just stunned by the cold, waiting for the first ray of sun to reclaim its wings. She watched until it made it past the rock to the point where the separated streams merged. She spoke at that point, her eyes never leaving the leaf as it continued down river, disappearing forever from their view.

Kai watched, his hand resting gently on her back. His silence spoke volumes, a quiet anchor in her storm. She turned to him, the dam broke, the deep buried secret spilling from her lips, a torrent of truth long held back.

. . .

"I wasn't truthful about helping my mother that day I kept you waiting," she began, as if rising from a trance, her voice heavy with unspoken words. "There's something... something important I need to share with you."

Kai waited in silence, sensing the weight of her words. "Please, go on," he urged softly, offering his support.

"Two days before the hunt, I stumbled upon a man drenched in blood." She felt a mix of relief and fear flooding out as she continued, knowing there was no turning back now.

"What?" Kai asked, "What do you mean, tell me."

Two days before we were meant to meet, I heard something strange in the woods, like panting or ragged breaths. I thought it was a wounded animal so I went into the woods to see, then I saw him. He was covered in blood and mud and looked at me with fear in his eyes.

"What's your name?" I asked him in shock.

"Silas," he rasped, eyes wide with a terror changing into desperate pleading. "They're coming... Please, don't turn me in. I can't go back."

"Who?" My voice trembled. "I sensed he was from one of the plantations, and I feared what that meant."

His eyes were pleading when he whispered in short gasps, "They coming... help me, don't turn me in, I can't go back."

"Why are they after you?"

His eyes started darting around in panic, as if expecting 'they' to come out of the shadows and grab him. "I run away. Mr. Thomas and his patrol, after me," he panted, becoming more panicked as he spoke. "They'll kill me."

Runaway. The word confirmed my deepest fear. I was conflicted, like Maami was the night before she signed the treaty with the British. We were the last holdout. She could not sign it when it forbids us to help runaways. She eventually signed because the treaty secured our land and freedom. But signing it came with a heavy price, one she struggles with to this day. Helping this runaway could change everything, it could reignite the war we bled to escape. But, when I saw the terror in his eyes, I finally understood Maami's conflict, we gained freedom at the price of our brothers. All Silas wants is a taste of what we have. I had to help him.

Kai was silent the entire time... watching her... processing everything he heard. He knew where this was headed had dangerous implications. "What did you do?"

"I helped him. I gave him water, found herbs Maami used during battles, and I bound his wounds with pieces from my skirt. We heard voices in the distance. They were coming and they were not very far. Fear and terror returned to his eyes."

I knew I had to take action, to somehow pull them off his trail. "You must hide," I commanded, my voice cracking but firm. "Be quiet."

The panic returned to his eyes as he grabbed my arm. "What are you doing? Don't leave."

"Trust me, I'll come back, no time to explain" I was on the verge of tears, but I choked them back. I saw determination return to his face and eyes. He didn't say another word. I helped him towards a fallen log under some low-hanging branches and told him to lay down. I covered him with branches the best I could, his eyes watching me the entire time. "I'll be back," I whispered, then I left.

I walked towards the voices, with no plan, just the desperate need to buy him time. Then I realized I was close to the ravine. The trail leading to it was just ahead. From there it's a short walk to the ravine, where the trail turns and runs along the edge. I ran.

Reaching the edge, I gathered rocks and logs, a makeshift avalanche waiting to trigger. Then I waited, the agonizing silence broken only by my exhausted breaths.

The ravine is about 20 ft deep, with caves at the bottom. If I could make them think Silas fell, or found a way down, they would direct their search at the bottom.

The voices were closer. When they were near the path junction, I shoved the pile over the edge, it made a thunderous noise breaking the silence. I scrambled into the bushes, my fear pushing me deeper into the woods. I waited and watched.

Shouts erupted, they were cursing making their way to the direction of the sound. They scrambled along the ravine's edge, peering down, searching for him. There were four of them. One bellowed, "Nothing here!" Another snarled, "Shut up and keep looking!" This voice spoke with authority, likely the leader from the way he was barking orders like a crazy dog.

Two men disappeared over the edge as they clambered down. One yelled about caves, my plan seemed to be working. The leader bellowed orders, sending one man back for more men and dogs, then followed the others down.

It felt like an eternity. Every rustle of leaves, every snap of a twig, sent me diving for cover. Finally, after what felt like a lifetime, I emerged from my hiding place, legs trembling like a newborn donkey. My heart filled with hope. I made my way back to Silas, praying he was safe and praying that I hadn't made things worse for all of us.

"It's me," I whispered when I arrived. I removed the branches as his eyes darted around, trying to confirm no one came with me. "We must hurry, we have to leave."

"Where're we going?" he asked worriedly, as I made a stretcher out of branches and vines like Maami taught me.

"Somewhere you'll be safe, now we must hurry." I helped him on, then we left.

Kai had been silent the entire time, and his prolonged silence added to Willow's growing unease. As she mulled over her decision, doubts crept in. "Was I wrong in telling him?" she thought, her mind racing with worry. She feared Kai's reaction, concerned that he might be angry that she had now involved him.

Willow knew that by helping Silas, she had broken the terms of the Treaty—a serious offense. The right response would have been to turn him in, and by confiding in Kai, she had made him complicit if he didn't report it.

"I'm sorry," Willow said, her voice cracking as she struggled to express her regret. "I struggled with telling you, and now I regret that I did. You're now caught in it too if you don't report it, and that's the last thing I ever wanted. This is my problem, I won't let it drag you down with it. Just know, your secret is safe with me, always. No one will ever know I told you."

He stared at her, brow furrowed, as he processed her words. "Walk away?" His voice conveyed the confusion he felt, that she even considered such a thing. "This is our problem, not yours alone. Now, where did you take him?"

Relief swept over her. Willow replied, gasping for breath, her voice trembling with relief and exhaustion. "By the Caves of Cemi-Ku. I took him to one that is not well known."

Kai reached out and held her hand. "That's way above the Swift River, it must have been difficult by yourself."

"I took the secret trails of our warriors," Willow explained.

"They're a lot shorter than the main ones."

"Is he still there?"

"Yes, but I haven't seen him since I took him food, the day I kept you waiting. I left him enough for 3 days, so I really need to go back today."

He squeezed her hand, his grip firm and reassuring. "Okay, we'll go together, but I need to go home today. They'll be wondering what happened at the hunt. We'll go tomorrow when I get back. Promise me you will wait for me and not go by yourself."

"I will wait," Willow promised, visibly relieved. She did not have to face the burden of her actions alone.

"I'll be back tomorrow a couple hours after sunrise," Kai assured her, his voice filled with determination. "I promise, and hey," he added with a hint of a smile, "don't worry, we're going to fix this together, alright?"

A flicker of hope ignited in her eyes. Maybe, just maybe, together they will fix this.

6

RUNAWAY SLAVE

As Kai walked back to his village, Willow's story replayed in his mind, stirring a sense of urgency within him. Helping a runaway had dangerous and far-reaching implications. They needed a plan. Silas could not stay in the caves forever and they would need help, but the situation was too volatile to share openly. Anyone who helped would immediately be guilty of a crime.

He thought about Willow's description of Nanny's distress, the night before signing the treaty. He understood the conflict she felt about signing an agreement forbidding assistance to runaways, worst yet returning them. He had watched his father, Olu, go through a similar struggle. He was eleven at the time. His father was angry when their leader, Quao, decided to sign the paper, and his respect for Nanny had grown tenfold when she refused to do the same. The idea of returning runaways into bondage was abhorrent to him and to add insult to injury, the paper required four white men to live in their village. His father could not bear the thought of living with the enemy. He wanted to continue the fight.

His father had never lost respect for Nanny when she eventually signed the treaty. There was far too much at risk. He had become less concerned about the clause prohibiting assistance to runaways; they would find secret ways around that. He concluded having white men among them was the greater risk. It was hard to keep a secret with spies living in your midst.

Kai's thoughts drifted back to the events of three years earlier, when the white men first moved into the village...

. . .

...It was difficult at first. A bitter pill to swallow for both parties—the Maroons were resentful of the intrusion, regarding them as potential spies, and the white men were wary of living among those they once deemed enemies. The first year was awkward and difficult, palpable. Both factions kept to themselves, but the ice began thawing when Sean Murphy, one of the white men chosen to live with them, found himself drawn to their way of life, enraptured by the beauty of the land. Sean felt a common bond—he too was a descendant of people who had been displaced and brought to Jamaica against their will. Sean would go out of his way to offer help or do simple things like sharing the wood he chopped or the corn that he grew. His simple acts of kindness were initially met with cautious skepticism, but over time, they were reciprocated in kind, forming a tenuous bridge.

One day, John Tomkin, another of the white settlers, perhaps out of ignorance or simply a lack of understanding, committed a grievous error. His actions, though innocent in intent, were perceived as a grave insult by one of the Maroon men, who wasted no time in voicing outrage. Tension grew as accusations flew, threatening to escalate into violence. Amidst the chaos, a woman named Aiyanna, stepped in, her voice firm yet gentle as she addressed the irate Maroon man. There was no anger or bitterness in her words, only a profound sense of understanding and empathy.

"I understand your anger," she began, in a calm yet firm, soothing tone. "But this was clearly a mistake. Mr. Tomkin does not know our customs, his actions were out of ignorance, not malice. We must accept our lot and learn to live together. So let's educate, before we condemn."

The Maroon man's fury abated, replaced by a grudging acceptance. Sean, watching from a distance, saw the entire incident unfold. He was impressed by Aiyanna's handling of the situation. Later, after the commotion settled, he approached, filled with gratitude and admiration.

"Thank you," he began, in a sincere and soft voice. "For intervening on our behalf. Please accept my apologies for Mr. Tomkin's behavior. We have a lot to learn."

"There is no need for apologies," she replied, her gaze meeting his, with unwavering strength. "We are all learning, each in our own way. What matters is that we strive to understand and respect one another."

A friendship of mutual trust developed between them after the incident. They began spending more time together, each enjoying the company of the other, each sharing their backgrounds. Sean told of his childhood growing up on a plantation in St. Thomas, where his grandparents had been shipped to Jamaica from Ireland against their will. They had a tough life, working alongside the Africans. Aiyanna listened intently. She had not expected they would have so much in common.

Aiyanna shared her own story of being a mix of Maroon and Taino descent, and the struggles her ancestors faced. Both the Tainos, the original inhabitants of the island, and the Maroons, descendants of African slaves who escaped from plantations, had fled the Spanish and found refuge in the rugged and densely forested terrain of the Blue Mountains. Her father, a Maroon, was killed in the early part of the Maroon war, and her mother chose to remain amongst the tribe.

Despite their different backgrounds, Sean couldn't help but feel drawn to her, viewing her as an innocent caught in the crossfire of someone else's war.

. . .

The scent of roasting yams, laced with wood smoke, permeated the air as Kai approached the village, yet an unsettling sense of foreboding settled over him. It was almost noon, yet the usual sounds of children's laughter and the activity of the noon hour were conspicuously absent. His instincts prickled with unease as he drew closer, a knot forming in the pit of his stomach.

Kai's narrowed eyes scanned the surroundings with growing concern, his figure blending into the shadows cast by the thinning vegetation along the trail leading into the village. The villagers had gathered in small, informal groups, their demeanor tense and somber. The women, holding their children close, were closest to him, while the men stood further away, their expressions grave as they watched a group of white men conversing with Quao, the village leader and the white settlers.

The hushed whispers and somber expressions of the onlooking villagers spoke volumes, confirming his suspicions that something was amiss. Kai waited until the strangers left before cautiously entering the village square, his heart pounding in his chest.

"What's happening?" Kai asked, startling the nearest group of women who had not seen him approach. The women turned to him, their faces etched with worry and recognition as they registered his presence.

"Manhunters," one replied, her voice tinged with fear. "They are searching for a runaway from one of the plantations."

"I pray for that man," another woman added. "May God keep him safe. Who knows what they will do to him if they find him."

A cold chill ran down Kai's spine as he realized the implications of the situation. They were hunting Silas, and with the treaty binding the villagers to aid in the capture of runaways, they had no choice but to comply.

Kai's gaze flickered towards Aiyanna, her expression a mixture of concern and determination. Now married to Sean and pregnant, she stood by the doorway of their hut, her hand resting protectively on her swollen belly. Beside her stood Kai's father, Olu, a silent force of protection. Kai's eyes drifted to Sean, standing resolute yet troubled amidst the villagers. His acceptance by the villagers was evident, their trust in him palpable.

The memory of Sean and Aiyanna's wedding flooded Kai's mind. Sean, fully immersed in the Maroon life, had become an integral part of the community, working and hunting side by side, earning their acceptance as one of their own. The wedding was a village-wide celebration, with even a delegation from Nanny Town, led by the revered Nanny herself, joining the festivities.

John Tomkin and Phillip Jones followed a similar path, readily integrating into communal activities and insisting on being addressed by their first names. While the villagers accepted them, a subtle difference remained. They had earned trust, but not to the same extent as Sean, who was included in matters of village security.

Milton Keynes, with his noticeable limp, stood apart from the others. Unlike his counterparts, he maintained a certain aloofness and formality, always insisting on being addressed as "Mr. Keynes." This self-imposed barrier created a palpable sense of wariness around him, casting a shadow of suspicion over every interaction with him. The villagers avoided him as much as he did them. Kai couldn't help but observe the cautious glances directed his way, noting the underlying fear that he might be allied with the British. Behind closed doors, some even whispered of him being a potential spy.

As Kai watched the search party melt into the wilderness, a surge of urgency gripped him. He had promised Willow he would return the next day to meet with Silas, but now the situation had grown dire. Time was of the essence, and he knew he must hasten to Willow's side to relay the news and devise a plan to ensure Silas's safety, but he must first find out more about what was said.

Kai watched as Sean left the group of men he was with to join Aiyanna and his father. He headed over to join them. His father greeted him as he approached.

"Hello, son. How was the hunt?" his father asked.

"Hi Da. It was good, we got the boar, but I'll catch you up later." There was no time to go into the sordid details about Taro. He turned and greeted Aiyanna and Sean, then asked, "What's going on?" Both Aiyanna and his father turned their attention to Sean. He was part of the exchange with the manhunters, and they too wanted the details.

"That was a group from the Prospect Plantation. They are looking for a runaway, called Silas. They tracked him to a ravine in the mountains above the Spanish River, then lost the trail." Sean paused, as the others waited. He was clearly not finished. "They want us to work with Nanny town to get our best trackers to help them find him."

Kai and his father exchanged a brief glance. It was what his father suspected and what Kai feared. He could tell what his father was thinking, by the subtle shift in his expression and body, the deep breath and the clenched jaw. He was bracing for a fight ahead, not a physical one but of wit and ingenuity. There was no way he was going to hunt and return Silas. Kai, he never doubted how his father would respond, but it was good to see it confirmed.

"Let's go inside." Olu suggested.

They entered the hut. Kai and Olu were offered wooden stools to sit as Sean continued.

"The man leading them is named Mr. Thomas. He is the Overseer of the plantation. I've met him before."

"What's he like," Olu asked?

"He is decent most of the time, but has a demon of a temper and holds a grudge if slighted. He said Silas assaulted him before running away... that's not good."

"What do you mean by that?" Olu inquired, his brow furrowed as he adjusted his weight on the stool.

Sean paused before answering, his voice laced with concern. "It means Silas is a dead man... If not by Mr. Thomas's hands, then by the gallows. He has already gotten warrants from the local justice of the peace for his capture. He will stop at nothing until he exacts his revenge."

The room fell silent, tension thickening the air. Kai had chosen not to speak, opting instead to watch and gauge how everyone felt about the situation. It was Aiyanna who broke the silence.

"We must help him." she said firmly, her gaze unwavering.

Kai and his father exchanged a knowing glance. They had anticipated Aiyanna's stance on the matter. She had always been outspoken when it came to matters of justice and freedom. But Sean was the wildcard, they had not known him as long.

"I agree!" Sean declared emphatically, his voice filled with determination. "But, we'll need to be careful. Milton cannot be trusted."

Kai and Olu regarded him with relief. Aiyanna remained unperturbed and resolute. They could tell they had had this discussion many times before, and had agreed on the position they would take, should something like this happen.

Kai and Olu nodded in agreement, relieved that Sean shared their suspicions about Milton. Aiyanna remained resolute, her resolve unshaken.

"I think John and Phillip would help us," Sean continued, his tone grave. "But it would be unwise to involve them. We can't afford to take any risks."

"And not all Maroons can be trusted," Olu added, his voice reflecting the complexities of the situation. "There are others who would disagree with the position we've taken."

"This stays amongst us then. It goes no further," Sean stated firmly, his eyes meeting theirs with unwavering determination. "Are we agreed?"

They all responded with a solemn, "I agree," a chorus of affirmation, a testament to the bond forged by their shared resolve.

"... and I know where he is," Kai said quietly, his voice barely above a whisper.

They all turned to him in stunned silence, their expressions a mix of shock and disbelief.

7

SILAS'S STORY

A heavy silence hung over Kai and Willow as they made their way toward the secluded cave; a large cavern hidden within a towering cliff. From afar, its entrance appeared as a natural fissure, a vertical split in the rugged face, blending in with no hint of the expansive chamber beyond. The flat peak of the cliff loomed over the fissure, its jagged contours resembling ancient gargoyles guarding their domain. The cavern's entry was completely hidden from the view of anyone standing on top.

The path leading to Silas's temporary prison, was a narrow and perilous trail, etched by centuries of turbulent weather into the rocky face of the cliff. Loose stones littered the path as it wound its way to the narrow fissure; an opening just wide enough for a single person. Each loose stone presented a hazardous obstacle, risking a precipitous plunge of fifty feet or more into the dense foliage below.

The urgency of their mission weighed heavily on Kai's mind. The gravity of their promise to Silas gnawing at the edges of his thoughts, overshadowed only by the looming threat of Mr. Thomas and the expanding search. He had hoped to tell Nanny after updating Willow about the previous day's events at his village, but Nanny was not around when he arrived. He wanted to wait for her before going to Silas, but Willow was anxious to leave. She did not know when Nanny would return and was concerned about his condition. They decided to go. They would tell Nanny when they returned.

. . .

Young Silas sat quietly under the shade of a mango tree. It was a rare moment of respite amidst the ceaseless toil of the plantation. The air was heavy with the sweet scent of boiling sugarcane, carrying the promise of "white gold," a term used by plantation owners to highlight its preciousness. He was only 7 years old, and assigned to the Grass Gang, a group consisting of other children of similar age, assigned to weed the fields and to cut grass and feed it to the animals.

Silas had known no other life. He was born on the small plantation located in the plains of St Catherine. His earliest memories were of being in the fields alongside his mother, Abena. She was his anchor. Her caring voice, a warm embrace and a source of solace and encouragement.

His world changed when he was 9 years old, when his mother fell ill. At first, she thought she had caught a cold, but as the days wore on, she developed a fever that refused to break, leaving her shivering and drenched in sweat, despite the oppressive heat. The whites of her eyes became yellow as she grew weaker, wracked by a deep, hacking cough that left her gasping for air. Silas could only stand by helplessly as her once comforting voice was replaced by the guttural sound of her struggling to draw breath.

She continued to work at first, with the assistance of herbs offered by the local medicine lady, but she began to miss work as her condition worsened. Her absence was brought to the attention of the overseer, the plantation was struggling because of a poor harvest, and every hand was needed. A doctor was brought in, but there was nothing anyone could do. She was in the late stages of Yellow Fever.

The night she passed was etched into Silas's memory. He had held her hand tightly, his heart breaking as he tried to find the right words of comfort. He was a few days from turning 10, and he wanted to be strong. He watched as her strength waned and her breaths grew shallower. With a last effort of strength, she whispered, "Hold fast Silas, the stars shine brightest when the night is darkest. Hold fast when hope appears lost. Find strength in that. Let it light your path." She said no more, and silently slipped away.

With his mother gone, Silas found himself transformed into a valuable asset for the beleaguered plantation. His youthful vigor and resilience made him a prime candidate for the brutal labor of tending and harvesting the sprawling sugarcane fields. However, mismanagement by the overseer had plunged the plantation to the verge of financial ruin. Faced with mounting debts and dwindling profits, the owner was forced to make a difficult decision: divest. Recognizing the limitations of his operation compared to larger, more prosperous plantations, he opted to sell and exit the business.

Desperate to maximize his profit as much as possible, he hatched a scheme. First, he would sell his most valuable workers, like Silas, at auction, fetching premium prices while detaching them from the land and the business. Then, he would sell the land itself, but with a significantly smaller remaining workforce, priced at market rates. He anticipated that interested buyers would base their offers primarily on the value of the land alone, likely arguing they could absorb the land and work it with their existing workforce. He planned to then offer the remaining workforce at a discount, seemingly sweetening the deal in favor of the buyer. This way, he aimed to maximize his profit from the sale by leveraging the perceived value of both the land and the discounted workforce.

The day of the auction was seared into Silas's memory like branded flesh. He had been thrust into a new role: that of a piece of property to be bought and sold. A scrawny, motherless eleven-year-old boy, as he stood on the auction block, his heart pounding in his chest as potential buyers inspected him like livestock. His mind raced with fear and uncertainty, wondering what fate awaited him in the hands of his new master. Amidst the chaos of the moment, Silas clung to his mother's final words; whispered to him with her last breath: "Hold fast, Silas. The stars shine brightest when the night is darkest. Hold fast when hope appears lost..." Those words echoed in his mind, a flicker of hope amidst the darkness engulfing him. Would he endure cruelty and hardship, as his mother had warned? The weight of his situation pressed down on him, a heavy burden for such young shoulders to bear. In that moment, Silas yearned for freedom, for the comforting embrace of his mother, and for a future where he was more than just a commodity to be traded and owned.

As the auctioneer's gavel fell with a resounding thud, Silas's fate was sealed. He was inspected and bought by an overseer, Mr. Thomas, an openly affable man on the surface, generally easygoing but harboring a short fuse that, when ignited, unleashed a mindless rage capable of great brutality. However, in the aftermath of his outbursts, remorse would wash over him, leading him to drown his sorrows in heavy drink and brood over his actions. Yet, amidst his regrets, another demon lurked within him—the inability to forgive. Crossing him meant facing his vengeful wrath, a trait that would shape the turbulent path ahead for Silas.

It was a long and arduous journey from Spanish Town back to the Prospect plantation in Port Antonio, located in the parish of Portland. Silas and one other person, purchased at the auction, were handed over to Jackson, another enslaved person performing the role of foreman of the slaves. He was the driver, responsible for enforcing discipline and work routines among the other enslaved workers.

Life was much the same as Silas was used to, and it did not take long before he settled into a routine. The days blurred into a relentless cycle of sun, sweat, and pain. Weeks turned into months, then years. Jackson's whip was a constant threat, but Mr. Thomas's reputation was even more feared. Silas had seen Mr. Thomas transform into an enraged beast, inflicting blow after blow on a fellow worker because he did not believe Jackson had done a good enough job enforcing discipline. The sight haunted Silas, ripping open wounds in his soul with each strike. Mr. Thomas had lost all sense of reason as a result of his rage; he was willing to inflict even more pain than what Mr. Jackson had inflicted. After such outbursts, Mr. Thomas would retreat into himself, drowning his sorrows in heavy drink and brooding over his actions. It was a dangerous combination, as it begged the question: what would happen if he was enraged while being drunk? Silas hoped he would never find out.

One sweltering afternoon, the air thick with the scent of molasses and fear, Sarah, a house girl barely older than Silas was when he arrived, was accused of pilfering a silver spoon. Silas heard the loud, gruff voice of Mr. Thomas, shouting to bring her to him. The venomous lash of the whip cracked against her slender frame, each blow tearing at Silas's heart.

As Sarah crumpled to the ground, Silas could bear it no longer. A volcano of rage erupted within him, and with a roar, he rushed across the yard and lunged at Mr. Thomas, tackling him to the ground. They grappled like wild animals, Silas landing a fist on Mr. Thomas's face before being pulled away by several hands. He knew his fate was sealed at that moment. The attack would not go unforgiven. So he fought with every ounce of his strength, breaking free from his restrainers, and then he ran.

The earth swallowed his pounding feet as he tore through the sugarcane fields, stalks lashing against him like angry snakes, its serrated leaves making thin cuts on his hands and torso. His lungs burned, his heart hammered against his ribs, but the haunting image of Sarah's lifeless face drove him forward.

The plantation had been his home and his prison for five years. He knew it like the back of his hand, weaving through hidden paths, dodging any watchful eyes that would betray his passage. He knew Mr. Thomas was a predator with a taste for vengeance, and would track him relentlessly. It would only be a matter of time before he was on his heels aided by his hounds, baying wolves with eyes like embers, following close behind.

The river, a ribbon of silver cutting through the green, appeared before him. It was his only chance. He plunged into its icy embrace, the current pulling him downstream, away from the plantation and anyone who was in pursuit.

A sharp rock ripped through his leg, sending a jolt of agony through him. He stumbled, gasping for breath, the water churning red around him, both friend and foe. But he didn't stop. He kicked, he clawed, his will to live a fierce guiding force in the swirling water.

Finally, the banks gave way to dense forest, the trees a welcoming wall of green. He crawled ashore, his body a canvas of blood and pain, but he had tasted freedom, and he was determined to never go back. He lost track of the miles he traveled. His wound was bleeding profusely, and he grew weaker with each passing moment. He had escaped the clutches of hell, and the taste of freedom, though laced with blood, was sweeter than anything he had ever known.

He was weak from the loss of blood when he finally found a dense patch of underbrush. He knew he had to rest. As he lay there with the sun high in the sky, Silas knew his journey was far from over. But he also knew that the fire of freedom, kindled by Sarah's sacrifice, was only the beginning of his journey. He heard his mother's words as he drifted off to sleep:

"Hold fast Silas, the stars shine brightest when the night is darkest. Hold fast when hope appears lost. Find strength in that. Let it light your path."

. . .

Silas, his features drawn and weary, sat opposite them in the dimly lit cavern, his gaze fixed on on the floor as he recounted his harrowing tale. Willow's arms, wrapped around Kai's, tightened as she drew him closer.

"...That must have been when I found you." Willow remarked, her words barely a whisper, more like a spoken thought.

Silas nodded, his eyes distant with memory. "Yes, I believe so. Your approach must have stirred me from sleep. I don't remember much, just that I sensed I was no longer alone, then you were there."

"How's your leg?" she asked, moving over to examine the wound.

"It's much better. I've slept a lot since you left and I've used the herbs. The swelling's gone down."

"How long have I been here?" Silas asked, with a puzzled look.

"It's been five days, Silas," Willow replied softly. "There is a lot going on."

A heavy silence settled over the trio as Kai absorbed Silas's words. Their situation weighed heavily on him, each revelation adding to the mounting sense of urgency. Silas's story confirmed Mr. Thomas's claims of assault, yet Kai couldn't fault him for defending Sarah, not when faced with such cruelty. He would have done the same, but Mr. Thomas's words carried weight, and beating a slave girl would be a weak argument to justify an attack on the overseer. He was thankful he was born in a different time, under different circumstances.

His people were also subjugated under the Spanish, but they had broken that yoke over a century before... Silas was still living it.

"There are some things you need to know," Kai began, his tone grave as he unwrapped his arm and placed it around Willow, pulling her closer against the chill of the cave.

Kai proceeded to update Silas on developments since Willow left him. He recounted what occurred the day he returned to his village, his words measured and deliberate. A shadow of fear momentarily flickered across Silas's features, as he recounted Sean's encounter with Mr. Thomas, the relentless pursuit, and the ominous warrant for Silas's capture.

"The Maroons have been requested to assist in your capture," Willow added, her voice steady despite the tremor that betrayed her inner turmoil. "We are required by law to do so and Sean believes Mr. Thomas will stop at nothing to see his vendetta through."

Silas's jaw tightened, a grim understanding settling over him like a shroud. He knew that adding the Maroon to the mix of manhunters increased the odds against him. The gravity of their predicament was palpable, with each word spoken a testament to the peril that lurked just beyond the safety of their sanctuary.

"I know that man. I have seen the demon that lashes out when he is angry, and I know what he is capable of...," Silas's words, steely with resolve, trailed off into silence before he finally voiced his deepest fear..

"He likely wants me dead." Silas declared, his gaze meeting theirs with unwavering determination. "But I'll be ready. I'd rather die than go back... which is probably likely now the Maroons are involved."

"First, we won't let them take you, second, not all Maroons will assist them." Kai vowed, his voice a solemn oath amidst the darkness that threatened to consume them.

"Yes," Willow confirmed. "We know others who will also stand by you."

Silas nodded, his gaze steeling with determination. Though the odds seemed insurmountable, the flicker of hope ignited within him like a beacon in the night, guiding him through shadows that threatened to consume him. His mother's words played through his mind: "Hold fast when hope appears lost."

"But we need to be cautious," Kai continued, his tone grave as he emphasized the gravity of their situation. "The stakes are higher than ever. The Maroon men have been instructed to travel in groups, never alone. There are now multiple groups searching, and there's a risk a lone Maroon could be mistaken for you, especially if they encounter manhunters not led by Mr. Thomas, the only hunter who knows you."

8

MANHUNTERS

It was late afternoon when Kai and Willow left Silas in the safety of the cavern, leaving enough food and water for three to four days. Willow was happy, pleasantly surprised by his progress despite his injuries; his wound was healing, and his strength was returning. She had left him a supply of dried passion flower with instructions to drink it after steeping in water. It would help him sleep, and sleep was what he needed most given the amount of blood he had lost. It clearly had worked.

As they walked back along the winding forest trails, Kai's thoughts raced with the task that lay before them. He was convinced that they needed Nanny's counsel now more than ever, but he was nervous about her reaction.

"Willow," he began, his voice tinged with a hint of hesitation, "I can't help but feel a bit apprehensive about our meeting with Nanny. What if she thinks we are putting everyone at risk? What if she believes we're endangering them by helping Silas?"

Willow was slow in responding, mulling over his words, trying to anticipate her mother's response. "Kai, I get it. She is my mother, and I know how intimidating she can seem. But trust me, she's very perceptive. She sees the bigger picture. I believe she'll recognize the importance of helping Silas, especially given the circumstances."

Kai nodded as he pondered her reply. "You're right, Willow. I trust her, and I trust you. We'll wait and..." But before he could finish, he stopped dead in his tracks as they turned a corner.

They both heard distant voices ahead, sending a chill down Kai's spine. He motioned for Willow to halt, his senses alert for any signs of danger. Peering through the thick underbrush, they spotted a group of men moving through the forest ahead of them, their movements purposeful and determined.

His heart pounding, Kai knew they had stumbled upon a band of manhunters, their intent clear: they were searching for Silas. Panic threatened to overwhelm him as he realized the peril they were in. Glancing at Willow, he could tell she was thinking the same thing; they had just left Silas. If they were caught, their mission would be compromised, and Silas's life would be in even greater jeopardy. What story could they make up? What if they were not believed? All these thoughts raced through his head.

Out of the corner of his eye, he saw Willow motion for him to follow her as she veered off the path. Her footsteps were silent as he followed her lead, navigating through the dense undergrowth. Every rustle of leaves, every snap of a twig threatened to betray their presence, as Kai held his breath, willing themselves to remain unseen.

Willow gripped the stone hanging around her neck as she crouched behind a tree. It was the one her mother had given her the day Taro faced the Council. She remembered her mother's words when she gave it to her: "Hold this, Willow. Let it be a reminder to tread carefully, to listen with your heart as well as your ears. And you, Kai, let your strength be a shield, not a sword. Protect Willow, but do not blind her to the dangers that lie ahead." Willow believed the stone held some of her mother's strength, and she willed it to keep them safe.

As they crept along the forest floor, the voices of the manhunters grew fainter. It appeared they had avoided detection, and Kai hoped and willed it to be true. They waited what seemed like an eternity before returning to the trail, vigilant and with purpose.

Kai was amazed by Willow's actions, her actions were instinctual and assured. She hadn't said a word, but he felt compelled to trust her lead. Traits, he thought, inherited from her mother.

. . .

Nanny wasn't a woman prone to idle nightmares. Her visions were heavy things, whispers from ancestors wrapped in shadows and smoke. So, when she jerked awake, her skin clammy and heart thundering, it wasn't fright that stole her breath but certainty that trouble was coming.

In her dream, she was in the jungle, its familiar sights and scents twisted into a terrifying tapestry. Thick foliage and hanging vines formed suffocating walls, and instead of the harmony of birds in song, she heard the ragged gasps of a terrified man. Her nostrils filled with the sharp smell of sweat and fear. He was running, stumbling through the darkness, each desperate footfall echoing in her dream-drenched mind.

Then the dogs came. Their low, menacing growls morphing into baying—sharp, bloodthirsty sounds that echoed off the trees. The forest held a new scent, of metal and cold cruelty. These weren't simple hunters. They were men with whips and chains, laughter a harsh counterpoint to the frantic sounds of pursuit.

Then, she saw her daughter, Willow. Always fiery and defiant, the girl's eyes were now wide with alarm. Yet, there was something... a determination there, a reflection of Nanny's own strength. A word echoed in the din, whispered breathlessly from Willow's lips, but she couldn't distinguish it from the din —"Si...," was all she could make out.

A stone, smooth and round, slipped from Willow's fingers, rolling into the darkness. As it vanished, so too did the dream, leaving only a throbbing fear that clung to Nanny even as the echoes of the nightmare faded.

This wasn't just a warning. This was the prelude to a terrible chase, and someone whose name sounded close to Si... —someone her daughter cared deeply about—was the prey.

. . .

Willow led Kai to her home when they reached the village. A wave of anxiety washed over him as they approached, not to the degree it did the day Taro stood before the Council, but nevertheless still there. Reaching the entrance, Kai paused, allowing Willow to enter first.

He was struck by its humble yet inviting atmosphere. A candle burned in a corner of the room, casting shadows dancing across a wooden shield and spear hanging on the wall above it. The air was filled with the scent of herbs, emanating from a pot that simmered over a fire in another corner. And there, seated calmly, was Nanny herself.

She sat alone, cross-legged on a woven mat, her gaze welcoming yet powerful. Her weathered face, creased with a lifetime of sorrow and wisdom, was etched with an unexpected solemnity.

Her eyes softened into a welcoming smile as she acknowledged Kai's greeting. She invited him to sit and Willow sat beside him.

"Maami," Willow began, her voice a mixture of apprehension and resolve, "I...we need your help."

Nanny tilted her head slightly, her dark eyes fixating on her daughter. "What's on your mind dear?"

Willow squeezed Kai's hand for a sliver of courage. "Maami, I met a runaway, a man named Silas. He was injured and being hunted. I couldn't just leave him..."

Silence stretched between them. Nanny's gaze swept across both young faces, taking in Kai's protective posture and the determined lines of Willow's brow. She then looked down at her own hands, her fingers slowly caressing the smooth, cool stone she wore around her neck.

"This stone," she began, her voice low, "was entrusted to me as a girl, just as I gave you yours the day Taro stood before the Council. It carries whispers of ancestors, a promise of protection in desperate times." Her eyes shifted to Willow, and her voice seemed to soften. "I saw you in a dream, daughter. The stone rolled from your hand, just as this one now rests in mine. Fate brings them together, and with them, a terrible choice."

Willow instinctively knew. "You've seen him...Silas? Your dreams show you these things?" her voice filled with a mixture of awe and curiosity.

Nanny nodded. "Two nights before the boar hunt."

Willow did the calculation in her head. That would have been the day she took Silas the food supplies, the day after she found him, and three days before Nanny gave her the stone.

How could this be?

"This man, Silas," Nanny continued, her words snapping Willow back to the moment. "His plight.... His life hangs in a fragile balance, and yours with it. I, too, once hid an injured runaway. That act nearly shattered our entire people." She hesitated, a flicker of doubt passing over her features. "There are those among us who'd walk the easy path, siding with the manhunters. Former warriors, who know these mountains well, but not the secret ways of my youth."

"Tell us what we need to do, Nanny," Kai declared, his urgency ringing clear as he recalled their close call in the forest. "The hunters are closing in. We need a plan."

Nanny raised a hand, a silencing gesture. "Patience, Kai. You have acted bravely, but to save this man, we must outwit them." Nanny rose from her mat. "The jungle is my oldest ally... We will use it to our advantage."

Moving to the corner with the lit candle, she pulled back a tattered animal hide, revealing an aged parchment with a hand-drawn map. As she traced the torn edge of the map, she spoke of its origins.

"This was shared with me long ago, a lifeline given to me by an old Taino priestess who trusted me and the struggles I led. See this ragged edge? It's not complete, it's a part of a larger picture, the Taino priestess said it was torn centuries before, the other half lost for eternity. It has served me well, yet there are places even my eyes cannot reach."

She touched the stone around her neck. "Like me, you both know what it is to stand alone, against what others believe is right. Yet sometimes, bravery happens in the shadow of secrets, not just on the battlefields."

Kai squeezed Willow's hand. Suddenly understanding the meaning of Nanny's words. The battle may have ended with the signing of the treaty, but the war still continued in the shadows, away from the prying eyes of the British. Rescuing Silas wasn't just about one man, but echoing an entire people's fight. Relief swept over him, Nanny was on their side.

"Now, come," let's sit back down. "Tell me, tell me everything and who else knows about this."

9

THOMAS'S HIDDEN DEMONS

The sound of the horse's hooves echoed through the cobbled streets as young Thomas gripped the worn leather seat of his father's carriage, making their way to his childhood home—a cramped, soot-stained terraced house on the grimy outskirts of Manchester, England. His father's unit was one of twelve houses, all joined together with common walls. The end units, prized for their single shared wall, were a luxury beyond Thomas's family and their meager roots.

Thomas's father was a formidable figure, a man who had clawed his way up from the factory floor through sheer determination. He harbored a deep resentment for anything that hinted at weakness, his booming voice and heavy fists leaving an indelible mark on the boy that Thomas would become.

Thomas grew up in a world of belittling sneers. His father's scorn wasn't just directed at him but extended to anyone he considered socially beneath them. From the factory workers to the beggars on the streets, anyone who failed to achieve what they had, was dismissed as a lesser being. Young Thomas absorbed this cruel hierarchy, internalizing a sense of superiority.

He hated criticism, it implied personal failure. Each stinging blow, each harsh word, from his father, fueled a growing bitterness within him. He became driven to distance himself from the vulnerability he saw in others. He learned to mask his emotions, a technique his father had mastered, while cultivating a certain charm reserved for those who were not perceived as a threat.

Within the cutthroat world of Manchester's industry, he carefully cultivated a duality. Those who questioned his authority faced swift and disproportionate punishment. Yet, he could also be the charming host, a benevolent figure, when the situation demanded it. Beneath this complex facade, however, was a simmering rage stemming from the deep-seated fear of once again being the powerless victim.

Amiability, wit and well-timed anecdotes, became tools of his trade. He could transform from a steely businessman into a jovial companion, particularly amongst the upper crust he now counted as associates, with practiced timing. He had come to realize that both power and careful charm could be used as a weapon and, or, a shield.

One day, during a tense negotiation involving a lucrative shipping contract, a competitor dared to question Thomas's judgment. A primal surge of fury rose within Thomas, his clenched fists trembling.

"How dare you!" Thomas thundered, his voice reverberating off the walls, triggering an involuntary twitch in those seated closest to him.

"You'll regret questioning my methods, you sniveling little..." He cut himself off as the competitor recoiled, a flicker of fear in his eyes. The shock of his own outburst jolting him back to reality.

A heavy silence settled over the room, broken only by Thomas's ragged breaths, as a wave of regret immediately bore down on him, like a heavy weight. He forced a shaky breath, attempting to reassert a semblance of control.

"P-perhaps I spoke too harshly," he stammered, a weak apology for the explosive display.

But the damage was done. His fear of vulnerability had been exposed, a crack in the mask... and that was his demon. He would stew on that moment, playing it over and over, deciphering where he went wrong, what he should do the next time to not show a loss of control. Eventually, he would turn to the bottle, and with each sip, each replay shifted from regret and improvements to what he should have done to that sniveling little...

Thomas's ascent in Manchester's industrial underworld continued, even as he battled his inner demons. However, he craved a fresh start, a new beginning far from the shadows of his past. It was then that he heard the phrase "As rich as a West Indian planter" mentioned several times by the upper crusts, igniting dreams of owning his own large plantation. These tales of wealth fueled his ambition, leading him to envision a future where his name would be associated with the wealthy barons funding industries in cities like Bristol and Liverpool.

Arriving on the island of Jamaica, he was captivated by its lush beauty. With the endorsement of a wealthy absentee plantation owner based in England, he secured the position of overseer on the sprawling estate called "Prospect." Here, he would reinvent himself, leaving the specter of his past behind.

Years later, when he purchased Silas at the auction, he saw a spark of defiance that mirrored his own. And when that defiance culminated in Silas attacking him, it ignited a festering fury. It wasn't simply the rebellion that stoked his rage; it was the audacity of a mere slave daring to challenge his authority. That audacity had to be snuffed out.

He sought comfort in the bottom of a bottle, but like his father before him, it only amplified the demons. Five days had passed since the incident, he had left the searching to the professional manhunters; the militia, the maroons and other specialist trackers. They were combing the mountain sides looking for Silas. But not a word of progress. He was incensed. His mind conjured horrific scenarios of what he'd inflict upon Silas once they dragged him back. The vision fueled his wrath yet did nothing to satisfy his hunger for immediate retribution.

"Silas," he hissed the name like a curse under his breath. Five days of Silas defying him, of his authority being mocked out there in the wilds. Five nights of drink; the demons being fed. He'd endure this waiting game no longer. If his men couldn't track the insolent wretch, Thomas would hunt him down himself if he must. He knew there was only one cure to his sickness: Silas broken, his spirit crushed—that was what would finally extinguish the burning rage within him.

10

THE LOST MAP

The air hung heavy and warm inside Sean and Aiyanna's hut, the windows tightly shut to keep out prying eyes and prevent anyone from overhearing their secret meeting. It was slightly larger than the typical Maroon dwelling and adorned with comforts Sean had introduced when he was still regarded as an outsider. How times had changed; now he was fully integrated, married to one of their own. Seated beside his wife, Sean cradled a clay mug, savoring a drink brewed from roots and herbs. To their left sat Olu, facing Kai, who was perched on the edge of a stool, his words tumbling out faster than usual as he recounted Nanny's dream, Willow's unwavering conviction, and the tattered map.

"The map she showed me," Kai continued, his tone softening with respect for its significance. "Had strange markings and lines like I'd never seen." He turned to Aiyanna, adding, "Nanny said it was given to her by a Taino Priestess, but it's not complete. She told Nanny that it was torn centuries ago, and the other half was lost for eternity."

Aiyanna's eyes widened, her breath catching audibly as Kai's words drew her into rapt attention, her hand unconsciously resting on her bulging stomach.

"Did you say 'strange markings' and lost for centuries?" Aiyanna's voice quivered with urgency. "Kai, please... describe everything about this map... everything you can recall..."

Sensing a shift in the air, an urgency far deeper than mere curiosity, Sean moved slightly closer to his wife, silently offering his support.

Kai hurried forward, fumbling for details under their focused gaze. "She seemed to think maybe there were ties to older ways... not like what Maroons use now, but... forgotten... maybe with ties to when your people joined with ours, or even before? Could there be paths they knew back then, that even time forgot?"

"I wonder if it's a map of the secret warrior trails," Olu mused thoughtfully. "Paths known only to those trained in ambush."

Aiyanna struggled to contain her excitement, her gaze shifting between Olu and Sean. "We need to see Nanny," she declared, her words tinged with a hope long dormant. "There's more to this... I can feel it."

She knew as soon as she spoke them, her words sounded slightly incredulous. They were colored by a hope not dared for in generations, but the others did not know that... she had to explain.

"Okay, I know this sounds crazy, but I think the map Nanny has is what my grandmother called; The Map of Trails. It was lost centuries ago. If it is, it may be able to help us with Silas."

They exchanged puzzled glances, intrigued by Aiyanna's words, yet still confused by what she meant. With bated breath, they leaned in closer, eager to hear the tale that had captivated Aiyanna's imagination since childhood.

. . .

The boy watched the strange objects loom larger over the horizon. "What's that?" he asked, tugging insistently on his father's shoulders, who was digging for cassavas. His father stood, and looked in the direction his son was pointing. He saw the mysterious objects as they grew, eventually morphing into boats, of a size that was incomprehensible. Above them were bulging sheets of cloth. He stood there transfixed as they approached. The father grabbed his son and raced to the village, seeking out the Cacique, the chief of the village, his voice urgent as he relayed the sighting. Together, they went to a higher vantage point, their hearts heavy with trepidation as they beheld the approaching vessels.

As the ships drew nearer, the enormity of their size became apparent. They were the size of small hills, their towering masts stretching towards the heavens like massive trees. The billowing cloth, anchored to massive trunks, were filled with the buffeting winds like pregnant beasts.

The chief's eyes narrowed in concern as he beheld the spectacle unfolding before him. "This be a portent of great import," he declared, his voice grave with solemnity. "We must prepare ourselves for the arrival of these strangers for we know not if they bring good tidings or dangers unforeseen."

The ships stopped offshore, so the chief sent a delegation to greet them in canoes, the size appearing as minnows alongside a great whale. The strangers dropped gifts of clothing and other items. They spent the night offshore, remaining onboard. The chief watched as they sailed away the next morning, away from the rising sun.

Later, he learned that the ship had stopped again, and the fearful local Taino Indians began throwing spears at the ships, their spears falling way short. A group of strangers boarded small boats and set off for shore, where they attacked the Indians, injuring several. The Indians fled, and the strangers let loose a dog that chased them, biting several in the process.

The next day, the Chief sent a delegation bearing gifts of peace to meet with the strangers. The act was well received, and there were no further incidents for the remainder of their stay.

When the ships finally left, the Chief was relieved but troubled for many weeks. He sensed the winds of change, so he requested a meeting of all chiefs of the tribal groups across the island. They met and agreed on a plan. The strangers could return at any time, in greater numbers, landing anywhere of their choosing. They needed to be prepared, so they agreed to share their collective knowledge, to the benefit of all tribes.

They called it the Map of Knowledge—a comprehensive guide detailing every aspect of their territory, from hunting trails to sacred sites.

It was unique, a single parchment divided into two halves. The first half, the Map of Trails, documented the intricate paths used by each tribe for hunting and travel. The second half, the Map of Sacred Places, pinpointed all the important places they would not want an invader to find, along with hidden trails to get to them.

The hidden trails leading to these sacred places aren't shown on the Map of Trails. Instead, special markers of unique symbols mark their starting points along the main trails. These symbols provide clues to where the hidden trail begins. A matching marker is located at the start of the hidden trail, as confirmation you've found the right trailhead.

So, the two maps actually work together. The Map of Trails shows the main routes, while the symbols lead you to the secret paths marked on the Map of Sacred Places. It was a clever way to navigate and protect the tribe's most important locations.

The map was significant because the tribes were scattered across the island. Each tribe had its own chief and inhabited different regions, often far from one another. The Map of Knowledge became a vital tool for coordination and defense as it allowed distant tribes to understand each other's territories and the routes between them. It enabled better communication and strategic planning in the face of potential threats.

The chiefs realized that they had to be united for the plan to work, so they decided there would only be one version of the map. The completed map would be entrusted to the Chief who initially encountered the strangers. They calculated if there was an invasion, it would likely begin where the strangers knew best. Additionally, each tribe would receive a map of their local hunting trails, marked with the coded symbols.

They also devised a plan in the event of an invasion. If the Chief thought danger was imminent, he would tear the Map of Knowledge in two. Runners would be dispatched to inform the other tribes across the island of the invasion and the coming threat. The half containing the Map of Trails would be retained for immediate use, while the half with the Map of Sacred Places would be sent to safety in the Blue Mountains along with a group of villagers. Should the invasion occur elsewhere on the island, that Chief would get a message to the Chief holding the map, who would execute their pre-agreed master plan.

Nine years later, one of the ships returned, damaged. They were shipwrecked for over a year, living with the Indians, who learned they were from a place called Spain. Everything was fine for a while, but eventually soured. The local Tainos had begun refusing to provide food so their leader, Cristobal Colon, called all the local chiefs in the region together and threatened them.

He threatened to call on the Great Spirit to issue a most terrible judgment: The moon would turn red, then it would turn dark, withholding all light. He promised this would only be a prelude if the chiefs persisted in refusing them food.

That evening, things happened just as Colon said it would. The moon turned red, then it turned dark, and all its light was extinguished. The Chiefs were scared and resumed sending provisions.

The Chief who held the map saw the demonstration of power as a sign. It was time to tear the map in two and execute the plan. He kept the Map of Trails and gave the Map of Sacred Places to his brother, instructing him to hide in the Blue Mountains. A number of the Chief's villagers, along with any others the brother could gather from villages along the route, would accompany him for their collective safety.

. . .

The chief's decision to tear the map in two lingered in their thoughts as Aiyanna paused, her gaze shifting between her companions. "The Map of Trails was never seen again," she finally stated, her voice weighted with the weight of history. "Three years later, the Spanish returned for good. They took our lands and made slaves of our people."

Olu broke the ensuing silence, skepticism furrowing his brow. "That's an interesting story, but how does it help Silas? The Lost Map of Trails is centuries old, and if it is what Nanny possesses, I doubt it has many more trails than what is already known... and those trails are crawling with manhunters."

Ever the strategist, Sean interjected, his tone thoughtful. "I believe we may be overlooking Aiyanna's point. If Nanny does have the Lost Map of Trails, then we have the missing piece to the Map of Knowledge. We just need to locate the Map of Sacred Places, and we know it is hidden within these hills."

Kai, wearing a puzzled expression, joined the conversation. "But how do you know it's here?"

"Because this is where the Chief sent his brother," Olu

answered, his words aligning with Sean's train of thought, the realization dawning on him.

"Oh yeah, I see." The excitement, spreading across Kai's face, followed almost immediately by a puzzled frown. "But, I still don't get how the Map of Knowledge helps us?"

Aiyanna leaned in to explain in a hushed tone. "The Map of Sacred Places reveals the Tainos' most cherished locations and the hidden paths that lead to them. Each of these special places is marked by unique symbols. Those same symbols reappear on the Map of Trails, an ordinary map of the hunting paths to the casual observer, but they're more than just decorations— they hold a secret message. Decoding them will guide us to the place on the main trails, where the hidden paths to the sacred places begin."

Sean added, "This helps us in two ways. We can avoid the manhunters who use the known trails, and the secret places could provide a safe haven for Silas."

Understanding dawning on Kai's face. "I see now. And it could be a safe haven for future runaways."

Lost in his own thoughts, Olu mused aloud, his words a quiet aside amidst the discussion, "It's here in these hills, but it could be anywhere. This could be like finding a single flea on a donkey."

The others glanced at him, the gravity of the challenge settling over them. The Map of Sacred Places was somewhere here in the Blue Mountains, but where? Finding it was not a certainty.

Aiyanna broke the silence with a tentative yet hopeful smile, her words carrying a hint of revelation. "I think... I might know where it is. But we need to confirm Nanny does have the Map of Trails."

"How... where?" Sean blurted out, mirroring the group's confusion.

"I can't say yet, not until I'm sure. But I believe I have a lead. Just give me some time," Aiyanna replied, her voice firm.

Respecting her wishes, they agreed to reconvene the next day. They would hammer out the details then meet with Nanny, who had suggested a discreet meeting spot to avoid suspicion.

Sean rose to see Kai and Olu out. As he opened the door, the weak, warm light of a lamp spilled into the yard, briefly highlighting a shadowy figure pressed against the side of the house, outside their view. The figure quickly ducked, dissolving into the dark shadows, unseen and unheard.

As Kai and Olu departed, a sense of unease settled over Olu, a seasoned hunter and warrior. He paused, senses alert, scanning his surroundings for any sign of danger. Satisfied, yet still wary, he continued on.

11

THE SHADOWY FIGURE

That same night Willow crept tentatively through the unfamiliar surroundings, the air thick with the acrid smell of putrefying flesh. Everything seemed distorted, as if viewed through murky lenses, and a sense of unease gripped her with every step. The passage grew tighter with each forward movement, the walls closing in around her. She could go no further; fear replaced unease as she realized she wasn't just lost, she was trapped. She stopped, pressing her back against the cold stone wall, her knees pulled tightly to her chest.

A primal instinct seized her, a silent scream of alarm that she was not alone in the overwhelming darkness. The feeling intensified with each passing moment, as if an invisible observer was fixated on her every move, but she could see no one. She glanced left, then right, repeatedly, searching for the source of her foreboding, but only the emptiness of the darkness stared back.

Suddenly, a flicker of movement caught her eye, a shadow darting in the periphery of her vision. A sense of dread overwhelmed her, so palpable that she felt like she was suffocating.

Willow woke with a start, gasping for air, her body awash with perspiration. Silence enveloped the room, broken only by the distant sounds of nocturnal creatures.

Willow could not shake a sense of foreboding since the dream. It must have been sometime after midnight, judging from the chill in the room and the brightness of the moon. She had been awake since; her mind actively replaying each scene trying to unearth a meaning.

She was sitting where she had sat with Kai the day before when Nanny walked in. The sun was just beginning to awaken, casting a gray hue over the trees.

"You're up early," Nanny commented. It was normal for her to be up at this hour, but unusual for Willow.

Willow remained silent, lost in thought, as Nanny began her routine of making a fire.

"I had a bad dream, and I can't shake the feeling that it means something." Willow stated.

Nanny looked at her inquiringly, sensing her distress. "Tell me."

Willow described the dream: the narrow passage closing in, the overwhelming sense of dread, the feeling of being trapped and watched.

Looking up, her eyes sought Nanny's, pleading for answers, "What does it mean, Maami?"

Nanny mulled what she had heard before answering. "It could mean nothing, or it could mean everything."

Willow was exasperated. She was used to her mother's riddled responses, but she lacked the patience just then.

"What does that mean, Maami? I could have figured that out myself."

Nanny continued unperturbed. "It could be just a dream, or it could be a message. Have you had dreams like this before?"

"I have had nightmares before, but they have never felt this real or as important before. I have not slept a wink since." Willow admitted.

Nanny sat beside her daughter, taking her hand. "Don't be afraid. I think this may be more than just a dream."

Willow's brow furrowed in confusion, curiosity sparking in her gaze. "What do you mean, Maami?"

Nanny took a deep breath, her fingers intertwining with her daughter's. "I believe you have the 'Gift'. Just like me. I've always wondered if you would, but this..., this could be an indication that you do, or..., or have the potential if you nurture it."

The revelation hung in the air between them, a quiet understanding passing between mother and daughter. Nanny recognized the flicker of recognition in her daughter's eyes, as the pieces of the puzzle started falling into place.

"You mean... I can see things, too?" Willow whispered, her voice barely above a breath.

Nanny nodded, her normally piercing gaze now an offering of reassurance. "Yes. I believe you have the same ability to see beyond the veil, to receive messages from the unseen. It's a gift that's offered. You have the option to accept and develop it or ignore it. In time, it will be withdrawn if ignored."

Minutes passed as Nanny allowed time for Willow to absorb what she had heard before continuing.

"I think, based on the timing of Silas and the dream I had about you, and now your dream, it was a message. I think it means someone is watching. You... and Kai... need to be very wary."

In that moment, Nanny saw her daughter not just as a child, but as a kindred spirit, a fellow traveler on a path of discovery.

. . .

A short while after Olu and Kai departed, the shadowy figure slipped away from the house melting further into the dense foliage of the forest with the practiced stillness of a hunter. They crouched, surveying the path behind them to confirm they were not seen, nor followed. Snippets of the conversation echoed in their head, but the pieces were disconnected, words but not full sentences. The windows were closed, and the chirping frogs were louder than usual because of the rain earlier in the day. A feeling of despair gripped them as they recalled the rain. It was a detail they had overlooked. Reaching down, the shadow touched the sole of their shoe. Ah, good, it's wet but no debris. They touched the other, and the feeling of despair turned to a touch of cold fear—it was caked with mud. They had left evidence...

. . .

Olu knew better than to ignore his instincts. He is a seasoned hunter, a warrior. His instincts had served him well during the war, saving him on multiple occasions; choosing to take one path over the other, because something about the first "just did not feel right." There'd been times, so many he lost count, when he heard stories afterward, of the ambushes lying in wait along the route he did not take. It was the same feeling he had leaving Sean's house. No... the feeling was even stronger than those old instincts. He had to go back, it shouldn't be ignored.

He tells Kai to continue home, he would catch up in a bit. He circles back to watch Sean's hut from the shadows of the base of a massive Guango tree. The thick leaves completely block the beams of the moon, casting a wide patch of pitch darkness beneath its wide canopy. He lowers himself against the roots, allowing the tree's shadow to consume his form. Breathing slowly and deeply, he knows he would blend with the form of the tree's flared roots. He watches as a figure emerges from the hut's shadow, barely distinguishable from the darkness of the night; melting into the tangle of root and vine at the forest's edge. His thoughts drift to the earlier rain; they could have left clues, but to check now could alert the intruder they had been seen. He would return in the morning to check. It was unlikely they would return and risk being seen in the vicinity.

. . .

Aiyanna had had a restless night after the meeting, her mind ceaselessly replaying the conversations about the map. Something about the symbols, brought back snippets of memories that had been buried for years. A memory of one particular visit played on the edges of her consciousness, refusing to emerge from the enveloping fog. She was sure it was important... but, what was it?

She was transported back in time on a whirlwind of memories and emotions. She couldn't shake the memory of her grandmother's death, and the pain of losing her at the tender age of 11. It felt as if an organ had been wrenched from her body, leaving behind a void that no amount of time could ever fill.

The night of the funeral, Aiyanna's mother had sat with her, and in a hushed voice revealed the truth of their ancestry. They were descendants of the brother of a great Taino chief, who, centuries before, had been sent into hiding with others of their people to escape invaders.

But there was more to the story, a darker thread to their family's past. Aiyanna's grandmother, a Taino Priestess, had been disappointed when Aiyanna's mother married a Maroon. She believed it tainted the purity of their bloodline. Yet, over time, she had come to accept it, recognizing the Maroons' fight to preserve their lifestyle and freedom was as much a benefit to the Taino Indians, as it was to the Maroons; a noble cause worthy of respect. When his body was brought back bloodied and bruised from a battle with the British, her grandmother had stood over him, speaking in the Awarakan language, words of blessing and reverence, honoring him as a fallen warrior who fought to preserve the Taino heritage.

It was in the midst of these recollections, as Aiyanna's mind wandered through the unlit halls of her past, that the memory of her grandmother's hut resurfaced. The air, heavy with the scent of dried spices and adorned with various feathers and dried hides, enveloped her once more. She was seven at the time, and could almost feel the chill in the air and the crackling fire, the soft-woven blanket wrapped around her shoulders, as her grandmother pulled a faded parchment from a hidden pocket within her robes. It was tightly rolled, its content hidden from view, but her young eyes fell upon a curious symbol drawn on the outer corner, curiosity ignited within her.

"What's that?" she asked, her curiosity spiked by the odd symbol.

"This," her grandmother had whispered, her voice filled with a reverence that Aiyanna could still hear echoing in her mind, "is the heart of our people, little one. Where their spirit finds its path."

And as Aiyanna lay in the darkness, the memory played out before her like a scene from a long-forgotten dream. It was as if her grandmother's words had unlocked a door to the past. Nothing of her memories confirmed she had found the missing map, but she was certain she was on the right track. The parchment, the strange marking, and her grandmother's mysterious words; she was sure they were important pieces of a larger puzzle.

. . .

Kai, defying his father's instructions, had not gone directly home. Olu was always a guiding force in his life, and Kai's desire to emulate him ran deep. He wished he had his father's ability to read a situation, to sense the unseen, and he recognized his father's unease when they left Sean's house. So instead of heading home as instructed, he remained hidden, watching from afar, hoping to learn his father's skills.

From his vantage point, Kai observed Olu position himself below the Guango tree, though the subject of his father's interest remained obscured from his view. Although Sean's house was beyond Kai's line of sight, he surmised it was the subject of Olu's interest. Kai soon grew bored, knowing his father's patient demeanor all too well when on the hunt. Eventually, he returned home, Olu arriving only twenty minutes later, offering no explanation for his delay.

Olu gently shook Kai awake. It was not yet dawn, but Kai knew better than to ask why when his father told him to get dressed quickly. They were headed to Sean's hut, and Olu briefed his son about the shadowy figure.

"Stay close to me," he whispered to his son as they approached the hut, "look for tracks, things out of place." They scoured the area around the hut and along the fringe of the forest.

"Look, that's a footprint," Kai pointed at a spot beneath a window.

"Well spotted, son. Let's see if there are any more clues."

Olu stopped to scrutinize the area beyond the tangle of roots and vines where the figure had entered the forest. There were telltale signs of bent branches and compacted earth where the intruder had stopped in the forest.

"He stopped there, to make sure he wasn't followed," Olu offered more for the benefit of his son's coaching than for himself. Twilight had given way to dawn when they finished.

As the morning light filtered across the village, life began to stir. Aiyanna's words from the previous night remained the central topic of discussion in hers and Sean's hut. She shared her memory, unearthed from a night of restlessness, with him as they got ready for the trip to meet with Nanny and Willow.

Sean saw his own journey mirrored in Aiyanna's family tale: her Maroon father's acceptance by her Taino priestess grandmother, from initial fears of diluted bloodlines to honoring him as a fallen warrior defending the cause of the

Tainos. Yet, he couldn't help but wonder if Aiyanna's mother also feared that their union would dilute their lineage.

Meanwhile, in Nanny town a few miles away, Willow learned the meaning of her nightmare and grappled with the revelation that she might share her mother's "Gift of Sight."

Sean was interrupted by a knock at the door, coinciding with the distant crowing of a rooster, heralding the dawn. Welcoming Kai and Olu inside, Sean noticed a change in Olu's demeanor since their last meeting.

"Someone was outside last night," Olu grunted, forgoing the customary morning greeting. The weight of his words hung heavy in the air, hinting at unseen dangers lurking on the edges of their village.

The atmosphere in the room grew tense as the implications of Olu's discovery sank in. Sean's mind raced, considering the possible motives behind someone lurking outside their home in the dead of night. A myriad of unsettling possibilities danced at the edge of his consciousness, each more alarming than the last.

"We need to tread carefully," Sean cautioned, his voice low and deliberate. "We can't afford to underestimate whoever this intruder might be or what they're after."

Kai shifted uncomfortably, his youthful bravado momentarily subdued by the gravity of the situation. "What do you think they were looking for, Da?"

Olu's gaze hardened with resolve as he responded, his tone unwavering. "Information, most likely. Whoever it was, they weren't here by chance. They knew what they were doing, and my guess is, it's about Silas."

Aiyanna, who had been quietly listening, spoke up with a sense of determination. "We can't let fear paralyze us. We need to move forward with our plans, but we must also be vigilant. If someone is trying to sabotage our efforts, we need to be one step ahead."

Sean nodded in agreement, his mind already strategizing their next steps. "We'll proceed as planned, but we should delay seeing Nanny. Kai, I think you should go see Nanny and let her know what's happened. Tell her we will meet tonight at the same place."

"Good idea," Olu chimed in. "I'll wait a bit then follow

after Kai. If he is followed, I'll know... and who knows? Maybe we'll get lucky and find out the identity of our eavesdropper.

12

WISDOM KEEPER

Silas crouched in the damp darkness of the cave, his injury throbbing with each heartbeat. Above him, the muffled voices of his pursuers echoed through the rocky chamber, sending shivers down his spine. He could only catch fragments of their conversation, but it was enough to confirm his worst fears—they were searching for him.

Fear gripped him like a vice, squeezing the air from his lungs in short, desperate spurts as he weighed his limited options. With only one way out and nowhere to hide, he knew that confrontation was inevitable. Despite his injuries, despite the odds stacked against him, he steeled himself for the battle to come, ready to fight to the death if necessary.

Despite fear, hope flickered in the promise of aid from Kai, Willow, and their allies. Yet, as the voices above grew fainter, doubt lingered. Relentless search parties combed the mountain trails, further stacking the odds against him.

Still, he clung to that slender thread of hope, willing himself to believe that they would return and he would make it to safety. But alongside hope, there remained a fierce resolve—to fight, to the death if necessary, to take as many of his pursuers with him as he could. In the darkness of the cave, he steeled himself for the battle to come, whether it be here or elsewhere, ready to defy his captors and reclaim his freedom at any cost.

As the echoes of the pursuers' voices faded into the

distance, a heavy silence settled over the cave. Alone in the darkness, his thoughts turned to Kai and Willow, his heart heavy with anticipation and worry. How much longer would they be? Were they facing obstacles? Were they safe? And amidst his concerns, he couldn't shake the haunting memory of Sarah, the young slave girl he tried to help. Was she alive, or had his actions caused her harm?

In the cave's silence, he prayed for their safety and Sarah's survival, unable to bear the thought of being the reason for any harm coming to them. Drawing strength from allies willing to risk everything, he waited for their return, ready to seize his chance at liberation.

. . .

Aiyanna's mother lived further up the mountain, on the southern end of the village. The path from Aiyanna's hut led through dense foliage and tall ancient trees, their leaves speckles of light on the narrow trail. She wasn't entirely sure what to expect at her mother's hut, but she had high hopes that her mother would have some of the answers she sought.

Her mother was given the name Maroya, by Aiyanna's grandma, after a long-haired Taino goddess of the moon, who as legend goes, takes on human-like form and comes down from the sky during the new moon to bathe in the Blue Lagoon.

She was a formidable woman of few words, with eyes that held both strength and a lingering sorrow. She was tending a cooking fire as Aiyanna approached. The smell of seasoned meats and roasting plantains filled the air, a tantalizing distraction from Aiyanna's purpose.

"Good morning Mama..." Aiyanna's voice held a quiet confidence. "Do you have some time? I have something important I need to ask you."

Her mother turned, a questioning look on her face. Nodding her head in acknowledgment, she gestured towards low stools by the fire. "Speak dear, what's weighing on your mind?"

"Have you heard about the runaway?"

Maroya brows narrowed in annoyance, as she hissed her teeth, "Who hasn't? It's all that people talk about."

"Many Maroons are helping with the search." Aiyanna, watched her mother's response hoping to read where she stood on the topic. She was convinced that she knew her opinion, but wanted to be certain what side of the divide she stood before embarking on the delicate topic she needed to discuss.

"Helping? They betray their own, that's what they are doing."

There it was, her mother's sympathies were on the side of helping Silas. She began to recount the recent events: Silas being hidden by Kai and Willow, her theory about the map Nanny possessed and the pressing need to locate the missing half to help them evade danger. As she spoke, conviction strengthened her voice.

As Maroya began speaking, her voice remained calm, but there was a flicker of recognition in her eyes. "Aiyanna," she began, "your grandmother... She was a woman of secrets. A wisdom keeper. Her ways were not always for me to understand."

"But Mama, I know... I know she entrusted important knowledge to you..." Aiyanna's words held a quiet urgency and a tinge of frustration. "...and with this threat... did your mother leave any instructions? Anything that might point us towards... towards finding it?"

Maroya sighed, a long, drawn-out breath. "She did. Years ago, she gave me a task—to hide away something of vital importance for our people, a part of a greater legacy. She impressed upon me the need for secrecy... to safeguard it until... until the time was right."

Aiyanna's eyes widened. "Mama... was it a map? Did she have the missing part of the Map of Knowledge?"

Her mother nodded slowly. "It was carefully wrapped, its contents hidden. She spoke of protecting places of great significance to our ancestors."

Relief and excitement surged through Aiyanna as she absorbed her mother's confirmation.

"Mama," Aiyanna continued, her voice catching with anticipation, "There might be a way to know for sure. There's a memory, a fragment from when I was small. I was with my grandmother and she had a parchment..."

She recounted the memory of the parchment, the strange symbol, and her grandmother's words. Maroya listened intently, her eyes locked on Aiyanna's. A flicker of recognition ignited within them, quickly doused by a blanket of sorrow and regret. After a pregnant pause filled with unspoken thoughts, Maroya responded.

"Aiyanna," Maroya began, her voice barely above a whisper, "your grandmother... she placed a great trust in me. Not just with the safekeeping of the map, but with something she sensed you would one day need."

Intrigued, Aiyanna leaned forward. "What was that?"

Maroya took a deep breath, her eyes shimmering with a mix of pride and sorrow. "The day she entrusted the map to me, your grandmother spoke of your spirit, your connection to the old ways. She asked... she asked me to consider becoming her successor, a wisdom keeper for our people." Maroya's voice broke slightly. "I... I told her I wasn't worthy."

A pang of sympathy echoed in Aiyanna's chest. She saw the vulnerability beneath her mother's stoic facade.

"She accepted my decision," Maroya continued, "but not without a final prophecy. She said that you, Aiyanna, possessed the wisdom, courage, and spirit needed to lead our people. I was to be the bridge, the guardian, until you were ready. I asked how would I know when you are ready? She said I would know when that time comes because you will come searching. "And I believe..." Maroya's voice trailed off, then grew steadier. "I believe that time has come. This moment, your search for the map... this is what she foresaw."

Awed silence filled the space between them.

Aiyanna's breath caught in her throat as she absorbed her mother's words, the gravity of their meaning settling over her like a heavy shroud. The revelation that her grandmother had seen her as a potential successor, a guardian of their people's wisdom, stirred a whirlwind of conflicting emotions within her.

"Mama..." Aiyanna whispered, her voice tinged with both reverence and uncertainty. "I never knew..."

Maroya reached out, her hand finding Aiyanna's. "I never spoke of it, my dear," she confessed, her eyes glistening with unshed tears. "It's such a great responsibility... I feared it would crush you."

"This must be why I've been so drawn to uncovering our heritage and why she taught me so much." Breathing deeply,

Aiyanna glanced around the room, "We must find the map," she declared, her voice steady with determination.

Sensing her daughter's resolve, a fierce determination mirrored in Maroya's own gaze. "Yes," she agreed, her voice ringing with conviction. "I have it here, but you must understand, my mother passed away before she could teach me anything about the map. When she entrusted me with the task, she saw the wisdom in you. She believed you would one day be the keeper of our people's knowledge. I was to be the bridge, the guardian, until you were ready."

Aiyanna nodded, absorbing the weight of her mother's words. "So, I'll need to trust what I know of our past and the snippets Grandma taught me," she concluded, her determination unwavering.

Maroya reached out, her touch a gentle reassurance. "Yes, your journey has just begun. You are now the Keeper of Wisdom. You have the essence of our heritage within you. Trust in that. I'm sure the path forward will become clear."

13

THE SECRET PACT

Willow couldn't wait to see Kai. It was only the day before that they told Nanny about Silas, and she showed them the map, but it seemed like forever. A lot had happened since then. The morning's conversation with her mother still played in Willow's mind. She had been told she possessed the "Gift of Sight," words she didn't yet understand. Nanny had entrusted her with the task of unveiling the map at the planned meeting with Kai and the others. It was a gesture laden with unspoken significance.

Accepting the responsibility, Willow recognized its implications. Her mother was acknowledging her as a kindred spirit and a fellow traveler. She knew the moment marked the start of a turning point in their relationship, a passing of the torch from one generation to the next.

Just then, a knock interrupted her thoughts. Willow opened the door to find Kai standing there. Her heart leaped at the sight of him; they hadn't had much time alone together since the day at the falls when she told him about Silas. Things had been moving so fast since then. She hugged him warmly and invited him in.

Nanny entered the room just as they were settling down.

"Hi Kai, I didn't expect you here. I thought we were meeting at the place we discussed," Nanny said, looking surprised.

"Yes, we were, but something's come up, and it's been changed to tonight, at the same place. I came to tell you and Willow about the change of plans," Kai explained.

"I see. Is there a problem?" Nanny inquired.

Pausing to gather his thoughts, Kai said, "A lot has happened regarding the map. It's exciting stuff, and I think you'll be pleased. But... there's more."

"We're being watched?" Willow chimed in, her intuition tingling.

Kai was momentarily lost for words. "How did you know?"

"I guess we all have a lot to share. You two catch up. Tell me about the map when you're done," Nanny interjected before rising and leaving the room.

"Let's go for a walk," Willow suggested, eager to talk to Kai alone.

As they strolled, Willow recounted all that had transpired since Nanny showed them the map. She shared her nightmare and Nanny's interpretation of it, but chose not to disclose Nanny's words about her possessing the Gift of Sight. She feared it might alter their relationship. Willow had deep feelings for Kai, and she knew he felt the same way, but this revelation was uncharted territory. She wasn't even sure how she felt about her newfound gift or how, or if, it would change her. So, she chose to keep it a secret, for now. She needed to understand it more herself.

Returning to Nanny's hut, Kai shared the story of the Map of Knowledge, while Nanny listened intently, clearly understanding the implications of the power of the Map of Sacred Places. Together, the two halves formed a potent weapon of knowledge.

Nanny excused herself, leaving Kai and Willow alone in the hut. They spent the rest of the day together, deepening their connection, while Kai wondered about his father's whereabouts. His father had promised to follow him from a distance, but Kai hadn't seen him since leaving the village. Perhaps he had found the intruder?

They remained together for the rest of the day, mindful of the covert nature of their forthcoming meeting with the entire team. Their rendezvous was set for sunset at the Caves of Scatter Falls, hidden in the mountains above the Rio Grande

Valley. Now that they knew someone had been watching, they were acutely aware of the grave risk of discovery. The consequences of being found were severe, not only for Silas but for all who attended. Taking extra precautions as they traveled, they were keenly aware of the severity of the situation. Nanny was absent when they left, but they knew she would join them there.

. . .

The anticipation was tangible as Willow unfurled the ancient parchment, each member of the group holding their breath. For Aiyanna, this moment carried profound significance—the culmination of years of searching for the lost Map of Trails, the missing piece of the cipher believed to be lost for eternity. As she watched Willow carefully lay out the map, the weight of her newfound responsibility as the Keeper of Wisdom bore down heavily upon her shoulders, a flicker of doubt quickly replaced with resolve.

With a sense of purpose, Aiyanna retrieved the Map of Sacred Places entrusted to her by her grandmother and passed down through her mother, who had served as the guardian until Aiyanna was deemed ready. She placed it alongside the newly revealed parchment.

The significance of their gathering was not lost on the group—they were bound together by a secret pact, a shared cause with grave consequences should they be discovered. Despite their diverse backgrounds—Taino, Maroon, enslaved, and Irish settler—they shared a common history of oppression and displacement by forces beyond their control.

As Aiyanna's hand brushed against Willow's while aligning the torn edges of the map, a silent understanding passed between them. In that moment, every witness to this moment was not just an individual; they were comrades united in a quest to continue the fight, to choose their destiny, and chart a new course.

The group gathered around the maps illuminated by a single, flickering torch. Aiyanna marveled at the intricate detail of the lost Map of Trails brought by Willow. The lines were worn with age but still visible, with familiar symbols she had seen on the map her mother had given her earlier. But how does it work, she wondered.

Kai and Willow had poured over Nanny's Map of Trails earlier and found something peculiar. They pinpointed the location of the cave where Silas was hidden. There was a marking, a group of strange symbols on the map in the vicinity, but the rocky path along the face of the cliff was not on the map.

"See this... this marking here," fumbling his words, Kai stabbed at the map, "that's close to where Silas is hidden, but the path to his cave is not shown. The symbols must mean something. Right?"

"I recognize the area and the trail," Olu observed, "But there aren't any caves around there."

Willow had been preoccupied the entire time, searching the Map of Sacred Places for matching markings, which had been burned into her memory since she saw it earlier. She was sure she had seen it somewhere.

"Found it! Look! Those symbols are also on the other map, the one with the sacred places, and it also shows the trail leading to it. But how does it work? The trail just stops on this map. It doesn't connect with anything."

They all looked, twelve eyes flickering back and forth from one map to the other, then back again. There was silence in the cavern, but the excitement and confusion were palpable. It was Aiyanna who broke the silence.

Aiyanna looked at Sean as she spoke, "I think it means they probably hid Silas in one of the Taino sacred places." He clearly had been thinking the same. He finished her thought...

"And if Aiyanna is correct, and I think she is, we have the pieces to unlock how the maps work."

Aiyanna's gaze shifted to Willow. "How did you find this cave, Willow?"

Willow looked at her mother, who had been silent the entire time, listening and observing. "I didn't. Maami did." All eyes turned to Nanny.

"You mean the battleground? she asked, looking at Willow. "The one where I watched from above?" Nanny hesitated, memories of the conflict washing over her. "The wild pigs, startled by the British... they seemed to vanish over the cliff edge. If I hadn't seen that..."

Nanny explained how she found it during one of the battles

with the British. She had set an ambush and had been lying in wait for the British to arrive. She could see the entire battlefield from her perch on higher ground. Suddenly, startled by the approaching soldiers, a wild boar and her babies ran into the opening and dashed towards the edge of the cliff, where they jumped. They disappeared, seemingly plunging to their death. A few days later, she returned to the area, searching, and realized that there was a ledge about 18 inches below the cliff top. From that vantage point, it just looked like a lone rocky outcrop, one she would normally have ignored had she not seen the pigs jump over the side. She scrambled down, only to realize that it was not just a rocky outcrop, but a narrow, rocky ledge that stretched along the cliff face. She couldn't see beyond where it made a turn, so she followed it and discovered the cave.

"From what I have heard and observed, I think we have found one of the places on Aiyanna's map," Nanny concluded.

"Isn't that something," Olu commented in utter amazement. Looking at Willow, then Kai and finally Nanny, he asked, "Did anyone explore the cave, did it have a back entrance or another path to it?"

They all looked inquiringly at each other.

"There were no other entrances from what I saw," Nanny said, looking at Willow.

"I searched the cavern, but there aren't any other entrances, and Kai was only there briefly, so he wouldn't know."

Kai, now the one who was preoccupied, said, "This is strange," as he pointed to two other areas on the Map of Trails, further away from where they had been looking. "These areas are far from the path to Silas's cave, and their symbols are different, but look here," he said, pointing to a specific symbol encircled on the map, "this V shaped symbol is included in the markings around Silas's cave. Does this mean... could they be connected?"

Willow immediately spoke up, her eyes wide with recognition. "That symbol is carved into the rock by the cave's entrance where Silas is hiding."

Kai could hardly contain his excitement. "It must be the marker for the cave! This symbol is the only thing in common between them, and it looks just like Silas's cave. See how these lines unlike the others, are grouped together within a circle: a vertical line which could mean the hidden fissure to the cave, a horizontal line above it—the flat clifftop, and the 'V' shape beside it could mean a bat, it looks like their ears."

The others listened intently as Kai continued his explanation. "These other unique symbols must represent directions or clues for how to find the hidden trails, leading to the same sacred place. This symbol confirms it—the cave has multiple exits."

Kai's words sparked immediate interest in both Nanny and Olu, both warriors who knew the tactical and strategic implications of Kai's find. Olu was the first to the map, but it was Nanny who spoke first.

"Kai, that's a great find. This could mean a secondary or tertiary exit. That would be a great asset."

Kai beamed at Nanny's compliment. "I think the one place that wasn't searched is the ceiling. That's the most likely location. Somewhere in the roof of the cave, there's a hole big enough for someone to climb."

"It probably leads to another cavern with two different corridors," concluded Olu, in a measured way, masking the excitement he felt welling up within him.

"There must be," Kai said decisively. "It wouldn't make sense otherwise. Look at the mountains here, they are high. This cavern, it's massive... has to break through somewhere, likely high up, hidden." He envisioned the roof of the cavern, rough and pockmarked with large cavities. "A hole, just big enough to climb through... and then... another cavern or more tunnels, branching off like rat holes."

Sean, who had been following the conversation, addressed Willow and Kai. "I think you two should pay Silas a visit tomorrow and search..."

"Now I remember!" Willow jumped in, unable to contain her excitement. "I was sure the other symbols looked familiar. I remember where I saw it—carved into the cliff face at the beginning of the rocky ledge!"

Aiyanna leaned closer, a spark of anticipation igniting in her eyes. "Did you see it... is it truly there?"

Willow nodded, anxious to hear Aiyanna's excitement.

"I think you're right, Willow." Aiyanna's voice rose with

anticipation. "The way the maps work is this: the symbol on the Map of Trails alerts you to a hidden trail, one that leads to an important site. The symbol on the hidden trail itself confirms you've found the right one. All you have to do is follow it! Now, the only missing piece is figuring out the symbol's meaning. It hides a message, instructions on how to find the hidden trail. With this symbol, we can work to decipher it."

Nanny rose from the rock where she was sitting. "Good, now for something just as important. We need a plan to draw the search party away from our escape route when we are ready to move Silas." She looked at Olu, who responded without being asked any questions. They clearly had been in communication on the topic.

He looked at the group. "Nanny told me there is a boy that has been sent on a journey of penance for something he did wrong." Olu glanced at his son, a flicker of recognition and paternal understanding crossing his face. "When we are ready, I'll set in motion a plan to draw as many manhunters away as we can, while we move Silas."

Alerted by the reference of a journey of penance, Kai asked, "You mean, using Taro?"

"Yes," Nanny replied, "but no harm will come to him. Jiro will take news to Crawford Town about tracks near the old village, leading up the mountain. Evidence like a fire pit and Taro's trail will make it believable. Olu will join the search to ensure no harm comes to him."

"And," Sean added, "I will ensure that Mr. Thomas's party is one of the ones that go searching. We need to keep him far away from here, when we move Silas. No telling what he will do to Silas if we stumble into him."

Kai whipped his head towards Sean, a mix of surprise and confusion washing over him. "When did you all plan this?"

"Quite a bit happened while you were gone, Kai. But trust me on the plan. And hey, tell Silas Sarah's okay too."

Aiyanna, sensing the tension, smoothly shifted the focus back to their immediate task. "Our job is to find a route and plan the escape... and in the process, I'll need your help to unlock the mysteries of the maps. You both seem to have a knack for it, especially you, Kai."

Kai tried to hide a grin at the compliment, a sense of renewed purpose filling him. He glanced at Willow, as she smiled proudly at him.

14

MILTON'S SHADOWS OF AMBITION

Aiyanna had a multitude of questions for Nanny about the origin of her map, while Nanny and Willow had their own for Aiyanna. Since they hadn't been present during Aiyanna's briefing to the others, they lingered in the cave while the others waited outside, allowing them extra time to exchange information and catch up.

The moon hid behind a cloud, casting inky darkness across the landscape as Kai, Olu and Sean exited. A chill hung in the air, carrying the scent of damp earth and the fragrant Jamaican Lady of the Night, its flowers releasing a clove-like scent infused with hints of citrus."

The night creatures were in full chorus as Kai turned to his father and asked, "So did you see anyone following me after I left for Nanny's? You never arrived."

"I did," Olu replied. "There was definitely someone shadowing you. They kept their distance well and watched you as you knocked on Nanny's door."

"Did you recognize him?" Sean asked.

"No, I couldn't make out who he was; he was pretty good at sticking to the shadows. I stuck with him till he got back to the town. It would have been too obvious to follow him further."

I heard something that may help, Sean interjected, "I spent the day with John and Phillip, trying to gather information, they said the militia is now involved with the hunt, so things are heating up. Oh..., and Phillip said he saw Milton snooping around your house."

"Our house? Milton?" Kai was incredulous. "Why on earth would he be looking around our house?"

"When did he see him?" Olu jumped in before Sean had a chance to reply, his fist clenched as if ready for a fight.

"It would have been while you were watching for Kai's follower," Sean admitted, clearly confused. "I never said it, but I was convinced Milton was the one outside our house last night, when you saw the eavesdropper. This information would have confirmed it, but now I am confused."

Kai was in agreement with Sean. "Me too. Milton is the most likely person in the village. We thought the eavesdropper would follow me, but if Milton was at our house, then who was it that followed me?"

Olu was quiet the entire time, his thoughts churning a number of possibilities but to no fruition.

He finally broke the silence, "We can't rule out anyone at this point; the stakes are too high. The person trailing Kai was white but he didn't have a limp. I would have noticed that."

. . .

The new recruit gripped his musket tightly, beads of sweat on his brow despite the chill of English morning. His heart hammered in his chest. This was it! He was just one among many new recruits gathered on the vast parade ground. He was finally here, participating in the induction process to become a Red Coat.

It wasn't just service to King and Country that fueled him; he saw himself a conquering hero in sun-baked foreign lands. A plantation of his own, respect, riches—the West Indies held a promise brighter than anything England had to offer. Better yet, why settle for anything less than the best? Jamaica, the crown jewel of the colonies, over twenty-five times bigger than Barbados! A land where boundless opportunities await a man of his ambition—vast estates, unyielding authority, and riches beyond even his wildest imaginings.

The training was brutal, a series of endless drills, barked orders, and grueling marches that left his muscles screaming. But the recruit pushed himself, determined to stand out. He was the first to charge the practice field, bayonet gleaming, always the one hoisting himself over the climbing walls fastest. He felt untouchable, invincible.

His superiors took notice. "Eager, this one is," he heard his Sergeant mutter to an aid, but he missed the hint of sarcasm in his voice and the smirk on his face as he said it. The recruit mistook it for approval. After all, wasn't it a soldier's duty to be bold, to strike fear into the enemy?

The mock battles, however, proved a rude awakening. He was so driven to prove himself, he was blinded to any strategy beyond a headlong assault. Time and again, his rash charges led his squad stumbling into traps.

"Milton! A soldier ain't worth his salt if he's six feet under, lad," his sergeant growled during one particularly embarrassing debriefing. "Think before you act, or those grand dreams of yours will be buried in some blasted jungle quicker than you can blink."

Milton chafed at the criticism, he would prove his sergeant wrong one day. The ships bound for the West Indies loomed on his horizon, and with them the chance to prove himself a hero. The sergeant would eat his words.

As the monstrous ship finally groaned to a halt against the dock after weeks at sea, a wave of awe washed over Milton. He felt small as his eyes beheld the immensity of the mountains, a rugged wilderness of green unlike the neat stone walls and rolling hills of his home in Yorkshire. He saw his future: he'd be a decorated officer within a year or two, then a politician after leaving the service, amassing power and wealth and the owner of a large plantation—the world was his for the taking. This was his promised land; it was the threshold to his destiny.

His first few weeks were a whirlwind of basic training; relentless drilling designed to acquaint him with the terrain and conditions and weapons handling, such as loading and firing muskets with sweat-slicked hands. Milton's eagerness made him stand out, but also led to more than a few reprimands. His impatience to prove himself clashed with the cautious strategies emphasized by his superiors.

He was finally assigned to active duty in a platoon under the command of Lieutenant Phillip Thicknesse. Their mission was to find the legendary Maroon leader, Quao, in the treacherous Spanish River valley. His unit was advancing along the banks of the river when orders were given to hold their position. Lt. Thicknesse, knowing the surroundings, realized that if they kept moving forward, hugging the riverbank, they'd be trapped in a natural chokepoint, where the river made a bend with land rising sharply on either side. He halted his men, sending two groups to scale the slopes, two to each bank, while the rest kept their distance away from the bend. He'd give them time, let his men gain the high ground before advancing.

Milton, however, could barely contain his excitement, he was finally in the battle, his impatience boiling with each passing minute. A flicker of movement caught his eye on the far bank, just at the bend—not the flash of red that signified his own men. He could not believe his luck, finally his chance to prove himself. He knew someone was over there he had to take action before or he got away.

He began a slow crawl forward, rifle aimed. His comrades hissed at him to wait and follow orders, but Milton saw his moment. He could already hear the tales spun upon his return —the brave new recruit taking down a seasoned Maroon on his first mission.

And so, as he crawled, his world erupted in a flash of lightning hot pain—a spear piercing his leg. He had been so fixated on his prey he had forgotten to check his flank. He looked over his shoulder and saw the Maroon hidden in the bushes where the river bank dissolved into the jungle. Their eyes met and held for what seemed like an eternity before the Maroon melted into the shadows as a volley of musket shots erupted. He had woken a beehive... then everything faded to blackness.

His next memory was waking in a hospital bed; the spear had shattered the bone in his leg and, at the same time, shattered his ambitions. He didn't remember much, but the face of the Maroon that snuffed his dreams was indelibly printed in his mind. He never recovered sufficiently to rejoin his unit and was discharged from military service because of the injury. He learned later that his action had triggered a battle, wounding one of his comrades.

His dreams of advancement shattered, Milton nursed a

bitter resentment towards those he blamed for his misfortune—the Maroons who had orchestrated the ambush that had cost him everything. And when fate intervened, conscripting him to be one of the settlers among the very people he despised, it felt like a cruel twist of fate, a further insult to his wounded pride.

Milton was on his way to the office of the Justice of the Peace, at the time Kai arrived at Nanny's house. He replayed the events of his life as he approached the office, his thoughts consumed by bitterness and regret. His once-proud ambitions were reduced to ashes by the harsh hand of fate. He was determined to restore his integrity, driven by a stubborn refusal to surrender to despair. The situation of a runaway provided him a glimmer of hope — a possibility to rise from the ashes of his failures and forge a new path forward.

Entering the justice of the peace office, Milton's heart sank as he was met with the familiar sting of indifference from the clerk. His limp wasn't viewed as a badge of honor, it marked him as inferior, an object of pity and scorn, or so he thought. He watched as others who arrived after him were granted audience with the JP, wounding his sense of pride further.

Finally granted an audience with the justice of the peace, Milton recounted what he had overheard, the words tumbling from his lips in a rush of urgency. Lost maps, Tainos—the pieces of a puzzle that hinted at secrets hidden in the shadows.

The justice of the peace listened with thinly veiled impatience, his eyes betraying a hint of curiosity beneath the facade of disdain. "And what of the runaway?" he interrupted, his tone laced with thinly veiled suspicion.

Milton hesitated, acutely aware of the delicate balance of power that hung between them. "Not directly, sir," he replied carefully, choosing his words with caution. "But it's all connected, isn't it? The closed windows, the secrecy—it's not hard to connect the dots."

A flicker of annoyance crossed the JP's face, his patience wearing thin. He knew Sean, and of his marriage to a Taino. What he heard did not at all seem out of the ordinary to him. "Enough," he snapped, his voice sharp with irritation. "You wasted my time with wild theories and baseless accusations."

"Sir," Milton replied irritated, sitting erect, head held high, "I am a soldier who has fought for this country and was wounded in the process, I deserve a bit more respect."

Calling for the Clerk to escort Milton out, the JP added, "I know who you are Mr. Keynes, I know your story. Please do not return until you have something of substance to offer."

Milton felt a surge of indignation rise within him, the sting of rejection burning like a brand. But beneath the surface, a seed of determination took root, fueling his resolve to prove himself worthy of respect, to rise above the challenges and regain his dignity.

15

THE CODE: ANCIENT MESSAGES

Olu and Sean returned to Crawford Town after the meeting in the cave, while Kai and Aiyanna, eager to maximize their time with Willow and Nanny, accompanied them home. Nanny retired to a room in the back of the hut leaving them to make plans for the next day.

The marking believed to represent the location of the hidden trail leading to Silas's hiding place, consisted of distinct drawings. One was a jagged line, above which were a series of triangles all bunched together, with some overlapping. Some triangles were clearly defined. Others were partially hidden by those in front, with only their apex visible. The final drawing was to the bottom of the jagged line, closer to one edge than the other. It looked like a rectangle with a vertical lightning bolt through the middle running top to bottom, and a series of dots beside it. Off to the side, was the encircled symbol with the bat ears, they had concluded was the marker for the actual cave.

They spent much of the night diligently reviewing the symbols, attempting to decipher their meaning, but to no avail. They decided to tackle it in the morning.

They had all agreed that both maps were too precious a relic to be taken from the care of Aiyanna and Nanny. So the next morning, Kai made a detailed drawing of the section of Nanny's Map of Trails that appeared to be the location where

Silas was hidden, while Willow did the same with Aiyanna's Map of Sacred Places. They collectively concluded that having these drawings and symbols with them at the cave site might trigger a better understanding.

"I can't believe that these symbols were created centuries ago," Kai muttered to himself as he painstakingly tried to match each line and curve.

"Yes," Willow replied, feeling as though a channel had opened between the past and present. "It's like these symbols are speaking to us from centuries ago, as if they've bridged the gap of time. How did they even come up with this?"

Aiyanna explained the little she knew from her mother and grandmother.

"My people did not have a language like the one the British use. They relied on drawings and carvings of symbols, figures, and patterns. Each having a specific meaning, but unfortunately, I did not learn a lot about it. I wish I had asked my grandmother when she was alive."

Willow glanced at her then, sensing Aiyanna's longing. "If only we could go back in time," she mused. "But we can't. We only have Now, that's why we should always make the most of it."

Aiyanna was looking over Willow's shoulder at the map as Willow spoke. She felt a connection with Willow, such wisdom at such a young age, she thought, as she scrutinized the map.

"This symbol, for instance," she said, pointing at a symbol at another point on the map. "See the wavy lines with smooth curves; that could represent flowing water. My people called this island, the land of wood and water, so it's likely they would have stuck to landforms, rivers, rocks, mountain shapes, cliffs, and so on. My guess is this shape here," now pointing at the area close to Silas, "see how it is similar to the river, but its curves are more jagged. That could mean the contours of the cliff edge."

"That's genius, Aiyanna," Kai's voice startled them as he joined the conversation at the mention of the symbols.

Aiyanna continued, her finger tracing a path towards another distant point on the map. "Now these symbols here, they could be trees, but that would be bad if that's the case."

Willow began to see the logic. "Because it's unlikely trees

would survive for over 200 years, right, Aiyanna?"

Aiyanna nodded in agreement. "Exactly. Hopefully they considered that, but they may not have expected the map to be relevant two hundred years later."

"So if they used trees, finding those places would be a lot more difficult since the markers may be gone," Willow mused.

Aiyanna concurred. "Yes, it would. Though there are few trees that will live that long, even longer now I think of it, like the Ceiba tree. They can live for hundreds of years."

Willow admitted, "I've never heard of it."

Aiyanna clarified, "It's what the Taino's named it, some call it the Cotton or the Silk Cotton tree."

"Ahh yes, I do know it," Willow acknowledged, confusion melting from her face.

Aiyanna continued, her tone filled with reverence. "They are sacred to the Tainos and can grow massive, extremely massive. We used it to build canoes. But my grandmother said the tree had a greater significance. It served as a gateway between us and the spiritual world: a conduit for us to communicate with ancestors and divine forces. It was planted by Yucahu, the Taino god of fertility; its deep roots and towering branches symbolized the connection between the earthly and spiritual realms. We would leave offerings and conduct ceremonies, prayers, and rituals near the tree."

"So it's very likely they would use it as a marker," Willow concluded.

"Yes, and my guess is, any place on the map that has that tree would be extremely significant," Aiyanna agreed.

Kai, who had been scrutinizing the map based on the knowledge shared by Aiyanna, added, "Da told me Mahogany trees can also live hundreds of years, so that's another possibility, but it's also possible not all the shapes that look like trees are trees; they could be mountains. Look at this area here," he gestured back to the jagged lines in the area of Silas's cave, "the one Aiyanna had suggested was the cliff edge. See those triangles above the jagged line, see how they are grouped together. It could mean a group of trees, but it could also mean a mountain range. The way triangles overlap could be depicting the arrangements of mountains."

"You're right, Kai. That makes sense. Do you remember the

view from on top of the cliffs?" Willow prompted.

As Kai's eyes lit up, they exclaimed in unison, "The Blue Mountain range."

"It's a series of mountains. Their peaks look like triangles of different heights stacked together."

"Yes, and the bottoms of some mountains are in the front, while others are hidden behind those in front, just like this symbol." Willow exclaimed.

The excitement in the air was electric, with Aiyanna just as animated as they were.

"I think we may be onto something," she said. "I think this is a promising starting point."

"Yes," agreed Kai. "We have ideas about two of the three symbols. We should be able to figure out the third symbol when we get there. My guess is it's some type of landform."

Having learned all they could, they gathered all they needed in preparation for the journey to the cave. Unanimously, they agreed that considering her condition, Aiyanna should not undertake the journey to the cave. She would stay with Nanny and wait for their return. It was the one stipulation Sean had made as he left; he wanted to protect their unborn child.

The night before, they had solidified a plan: if needed, they'd spend the night in the cave with Silas. It was becoming increasingly dangerous to travel after dark, they recognized the need for caution. Their objectives were extensive, ranging from exploring the cave for the exits hinted at on the maps to deciphering the secrets governing their use.

With final goodbyes, Willow and Kai left on their journey.

16

HIGH STAKES

Milton straightened his coat, doing his best to hide the tremble in his hands. He'd been turned away by the JP, mocked for his theories, labeled a desperate fool. But Mr. Thomas... Now, he was a man of action, a man who would understand the value of the information he had. A shiver of excitement—or was it fear?—raced down his spine. This was a big gamble but he had to take the chance, so convinced he was that he was on to something big.

The rhythmic tick of the grandfather clock filled the silence of Mr. Thomas's study. Annoyance simmering within him. There was a light knock at the door. The nerve of it—interrupting him again! His fingers tightened on the quill, nearly snapping it in two.

The knock persisted, heavier this time. "Sir? Forgive the intrusion," the housemaid murmured, her voice faltering under his withering glare, "but there's a man at the door..."

"I haven't the time for peddlers or charity cases!" he barked. "And who is this man, anyway?"

"He calls himself Mr. Keynes, sir. Says he was a soldier, from, ...from England sir..." The maid's voice trailed off. "He says he has information about Silas."

Thomas froze mid-motion. "Information?" His voice was deceptively calm, the mention of Silas's name sending an undercurrent of rage through him, he was outwardly controlled, his whitened knuckles holding the quill was the only visible clue to the rage building in him. "Bring him in," he snapped.

The maid gasped, a flicker of fear in her eyes, before bobbing a curtsey and hastily retreating. He heard another knock, then the creak of the study door opening.

"Mr. Keynes, if you please, sir," the maid's voice announced before the door shut with a soft click.

Thomas leaned back, his gaze sweeping over the man who now stood awkwardly before him. The fellow was disheveled, his coat had seen better years, frayed at the sleeves and dusted with the white marl of the Jamaican roads. His eyes darted about the room, taking in the opulent furnishings with a mixture of awe and desperation.

"Well, Mr. Keynes," Thomas said, his voice dripping with disdain, "I trust this information is worth the interruption."

Milton swallowed hard, trying to steady his nerves. "It is, Mr. Thomas. I apologize for the intrusion, but I recently overheard... certain whispers in the village—regarding Silas." He paused, gauging Thomas's reaction.

"Whispers," Thomas echoed, his lips curling in a sneer. "Is that all you have? Gossip? I'm already drowning in gossip, I need hard, actionable information."

Milton pressed on, "It was more than mere gossip, sir. I also spoke to the Justice of the Peace. He refused to listen and dismissed it as speculation, but I believe you might find them of... interest." He took a calculated risk, "I believe I know who is assisting Silas, someone in the Maroon village."

"Dismissed as speculation, you say?" Thomas leaned back in his chair, steepling his fingers. "So you decided to bring your unfounded theories to a man with far more pressing matters than village gossip." His voice was a low rumble, his eyes devouring Milton like a predator sizing up its prey.

Milton met his gaze, holding his ground. "Not unfounded, sir. Just... unconventional. The Justice of the Peace wouldn't entertain the possibility of Maroons defying the treaty. But you, Mr. Thomas, I believe you possess a... clearer understanding of the realities on the ground."

A flicker of something unreadable crossed Thomas's face. "Do you now? Tell me, Mr. Keynes, exactly what kind of unconventional theories do you have?"

Milton took a deep breath. "There's a man in the village, a man named Olu. A Maroon from Crawford Town, known for being... restless, shall we say. He has a son, Kai, a young firebrand who wouldn't hesitate to defy authority." He paused, gauging Thomas's reaction.

Thomas remained impassive. "And how does this Olu, this restless Maroon, tie into the escape of my slave?"

"Yesterday," Milton continued, "I observed Kai leaving Crawford Town in a hurry. He headed straight for Nanny Town, another Maroon settlement quite some distance away." He kept his voice steady, leaving out the details of how he knew where Kai went.

"So?" Thomas scoffed. "Maroons visit each other. It hardly constitutes proof of anything."

"Maybe not," Milton conceded. "But what if I told you there were...whispers of a connection between Olu and those who might sympathize with a runaway seeking... freedom?"

Thomas's eyes narrowed. "Sympathize? Or perhaps see an opportunity to exploit the situation for their own benefit?" He leaned forward, his voice dangerously soft. "Maroons are known to be a cunning lot. What makes you think they wouldn't use this runaway as a bargaining chip with the authorities?"

"Because," Milton said quickly, "there might be more to it than that. Certain rumors mention... ancestral knowledge, knowledge passed down by the Taino people." He saw a flicker of surprise in Thomas's gaze, a chink in his armor.

A sneer twisted Thomas's lips. "Ancestral knowledge? You think I have time for fairy tales, Mr. Keynes? I want facts, not folklore." He slammed his fist on the desk, the sound echoing in the opulent room.

Milton flinched but held his ground. "Sir, I understand your frustration. But these whispers... They spoke of a woman, a Taino woman connected to Olu. Perhaps she might know more about his... activities."

Milton knew this was a gamble. Mentioning a Taino woman might pique Thomas's interest, but it could also backfire if he suspects Milton is grasping at straws and he couldn't afford to mention Aiyanna, at least not yet. He was hesitant to implicate

Sean, who had a good reputation and powerful friends. He was prepared to implicate him, but only when he had more proof, so he trod carefully with Aiyanna's name.

Thomas steepled his fingers, his gaze cold and assessing. "A Taino woman, you say? And what makes you think this woman would be willing to share her secrets with a complete stranger?"

"Because," Milton said, taking another calculated risk, "perhaps she has a reason to sympathize with a runaway slave. Perhaps she understands the yearning for freedom as much as anyone."

He watched Thomas's face for any reaction, any flicker of something other than cold calculation.

"Sympathy with the enemy? What foolishness is this?" Thomas sneered, his voice dripping with contempt. "You come here with half-heard whispers and tales of freedom, but no real proof, no solid leads that might bring me closer to reclaiming my property!"

Milton faltered under the onslaught, but a flicker of defiance sparked in his eyes. "With respect, Mr. Thomas, sometimes unconventional leads can be the most revealing..."

"Unconventional?" Thomas cut him off, his voice rising. "You've wasted my time with speculation and empty theories! Is this how you fought for your King and country, Mr. Keynes? With wild conjecture and empty promises?"

Milton's face flushed. "Sir, I saw... I witnessed..."

"Enough!" Thomas roared, slamming his fist on the desk for emphasis. "Enough playing at soldier, enough playing at detective. My patience is at an end, Mr. Keynes. Either you provide me with something of substance—a name, a location, anything that proves your wild claims of aiding Silas—or face the consequences of wasting my time."

His voice echoed in the suddenly still room. The air crackled with tension as Milton struggled to find the right words, his last shred of bravado wavering.

Thomas leaned forward, his eyes blazing. "You've got one chance, soldier. Tell me something I can use, or walk out that door and never return. The choice is yours." The threat hung heavy in the air, a silent ultimatum.

Taking a deep breath, Milton met Thomas's gaze with a

newfound resolve. "Mr. Thomas, you're right. I don't have the definitive proof you seek right now. But the whispers, the sightings—they point to something brewing, a network defying your authority."

He saw a flicker of something in Thomas's eyes—a spark of begrudging respect, perhaps? Or maybe a flicker of doubt about dismissing Milton entirely.

"Give me a chance, sir," Milton pressed on, his voice regaining its strength. "I'll delve deeper, gather more concrete evidence about this... this rogue group and their connection to Silas. I won't let you down."

Thomas studied Milton for a long moment, his sharp gaze dissecting the man before him. Internally, a war raged. Dismissing the man seemed like the easier option, but something about Milton's desperation, the glint of determination in his eyes, intrigued him. There was a chance, however slim, that this soldier could prove useful.

"A chance," Thomas finally conceded. "But a very short one. You return by tomorrow evening, with something more substantial than whispers and half-formed theories. Something that points a finger directly at those harboring my runaway."

He paused, letting the silence stretch for a tense moment. "Fail to do so, Mr. Keynes, and the consequences will be... unpleasant. Let's just say your wounds from that 'King's service' will seem like mere scratches compared to what awaits you."

The threat was clear, a veiled promise of violence if Milton failed to deliver. But it also left the door open, a small window of opportunity for the former soldier to prove his worth.

Milton swallowed hard, forcing a confident nod. "Thank you, sir. I won't disappoint you." He knew the clock was ticking. He had a day to find that smoking gun, to turn whispers into actionable information, and to gamble his very safety on a desperate promise.

Milton fought a wave of nausea as the full weight of Thomas's threat settled upon him. Being branded a liar, even violently punished... Those were horrors he could comprehend. But the unspoken threat, the veiled suggestion hanging heavy in the air, sent shivers down his spine. He knew Thomas was capable of far worse fates than public humiliation.

He forced himself to meet Thomas's cold stare, swallowing the fear that threatened to choke him. "I appreciate your... trust, Mr. Thomas," he managed, his voice barely a whisper.

A low, dismissive snort escaped Thomas. "Trust? Let's not confuse desperation with trust, Mr. Keynes. You have until tomorrow, no more. Fail, and you'll find yourself wishing for a mere flogging in the village square."

Milton nodded, turning on his heel and forcing himself to walk out of the study with a semblance of composure. The moment the heavy mahogany door closed behind him, his shoulders slumped, and the facade of strength crumbled. He shuddered. Whatever fate Thomas had in store for him...it was far worse, he imagined, than anything he had experienced before.

17

REDISCOVERY

The dense foliage gradually thinned as they ascended the mountain trail, revealing glimpses of the vast panorama below. Exhausted from the pace they had set, they stopped for a while to catch their breath and enjoy the sweeping view across the landscape. Willow grabbed Kai's arm, pointing excitedly towards the distance.

"Look, Kai!" she exclaimed, her voice tinged with a mixture of surprise and possibility. "There! By the cliff's edge, see that rock?"

Kai squinted, following her finger. He saw what got her attention. There was a weathered rock sitting on a mound on the cliff top, surrounded by green foliage. The rock stood by itself, like a sentry guarding its secrets, its center split in two like a jagged scar. A flicker of recognition sparked in Willow's eyes.

"I remember that rock," she whispered, "I've seen it countless times before, but never like this."

She had seen the rock on many other occasions, but the seemingly ordinary rock now took on a new meaning, its split resembling the lightning bolt symbol from the cryptic map.

"It could be," Kai agreed. "It does look rectangular, and the split is consistent with the symbol."

Reaching the summit, they emerged from the final cluster of bushes onto the exposed clifftop. The world stretched before them, a breathtaking view of the distant range with shades of greens and blues woven into the jagged peaks of the Blue Mountains. A cool breeze bathed them, a welcomed reprieve from the heat and humidity of the climb.

Willow unfurled a wrinkled piece of parchment—her recreation of a portion of the Map of Sacred Places. Next to it, Kai spread out his, a similarly rough sketch of Nanny's Map of Trails. Sweat dripped from his brow, darkening the aged paper in blots.

"The mountains..." Willow traced the row of clustered triangles with her finger, a sense of hope blossoming in her chest. "It's an exact match!"

Kai followed her gaze, his heart pounding with newfound confidence. He traced the jagged line on his own drawing. "And see here... how the line follows the contour of the cliff?"

"Yes!" Willow's confirmation fueled their excitement. "We're on the right track!"

But as their gazes compared the distant mountain range to the maps, a flicker of doubt crept in. The peaks aligned remarkably well with the triangles on the map, yet something felt off. They scrutinized the map, their gaze flickering between the mountain range and parchment. A knot of frustration tightened in Kai's stomach; there was one additional peak in the actual range compared to the map.

A sense of disappointment threatened to engulf them. They had been so sure they were close to deciphering the symbols. Just when discouragement threatened to engulf them, Willow suggested,

"Let's come back to this later," she said, her voice resolute. "Remember that unusual split rock we saw earlier? Where do you think it would be if we were standing right below it?"

Together, they analyzed the terrain, their combined knowledge of the area guiding their deduction. They pinpointed the location, their eyes meeting in a silent understanding.

Following their deduction, they went to the spot, anticipation building with each step. There it was, the weathered rock with its jagged split, a mirror image of the symbol on the map. They marveled at its size, the depth of the chasm too dark and narrow to see through.

"The split isn't even clean," Kai commented, tracing the irregular fracture with his finger.

"But it has to be the third symbol," Willow said with conviction.

Kai returned to the map, studying it intently. The features of the map aligned perfectly with the mountain range before him, leaving him convinced that the only discrepancy was the number of peaks. There was an extra peak in the actual mountain range compared to the map, but determining which one was the challenge.

Willow, meanwhile, with Kai engrossed in the map, continued to examine the rock.

"This is strange," she murmured, her brow furrowed in concentration. She moved slightly, adjusting her angle to the split. "Kai, come look at this!"

He went to her. "What is it?"

"I can see all the way through the split, but only from here... look!" She stepped aside, inviting him to take a closer look. He peered through the opening, able to see all the way to the mountains, but he wasn't sure what she wanted him to notice. "Focus on this side of the cliff, not on the mountains."

"Wait, what...?" A jolt shot through him. "I can see the area right above the hidden ledge. The place where you step down to the ledge and then follow the trail that leads to the cave. It is in the direct line of sight." He peered again through the split, and then, it hit him.

He stepped back, grabbing the map. One, two, three... he counted the peaks on the map, then glanced at the mountains, counting again. A frown etched itself onto his face. Something wasn't right. He traced the line of triangles once more, his finger pausing at the fifth peak, his eyes flickered to the mountains. It didn't match. There were too many in the real world... The fifth one was missing on the map.

Willow watched the pantomime of changing emotions across his face, a flicker of her own doubt mirroring his. Finally, his gaze met hers, a spark of triumph in his eyes.

"They left one off on purpose," he said, his voice barely above a whisper. "I think I know why."

He hurried back to the rock, confirming his suspicion as he peered through the split. Only the fifth peak was visible, and the hidden ledge was directly in the line of sight.

Exhilaration surged through them. They had cracked the code! The mismatched peaks, the strangely angled view through the split rock—everything clicked into place.

Willow was elated, but she had questions.

"What's the purpose of omitting one of the peaks from the drawing? I mean, all you have to do is look through the crack. That's how we found the hidden ledge: the lines pointed to the cliff edge, the triangles pointed us to the mountain range, and the third symbol led us to the rock with the split. The hidden ledge is in the line of sight as long as you are looking through the crack, in the direction of the mountains, and not away from them. It seems that's sufficient to find the ledge. That's how we did it."

"That's true, but they couldn't predict how the landscape might change. There could be other rocks with splits or even trees that could potentially confuse us. This split rock provided a direct line of sight to the hidden ledge. So, they chose the only peak visible through it and left it off the map. That way, finding the peak would confirm we were on track, and from there, we'd have a perfect view of the ridge above the ledge," Kai explained.

Willow finally saw the logic. "That's clever."

This discovery sent a jolt of excitement through them. They were on the verge of unlocking the code!

But a moment later, Willow's smile faltered.

"Wait," she said, a hint of frustration creeping into her voice. "We only recognized the ledge because we already knew where the trailhead was. Without that knowledge, we wouldn't have understood what we were seeing."

Kai immediately understood her point, and she was right. A wave of disappointment washed over him.

They both realized they were close, but still had a crucial piece unsolved. Kai stared at his map, his initial thrill replaced by a gnawing sense of incompleteness. Willow mirrored his frustration, her gaze shifting between their maps.

"These dots on mine..." she murmured, her voice barely above a whisper. "They're not on yours. Were they missing from the original map?"

Kai squinted at his map, a jolt of realization shooting

through him. He remembered being distracted by Willow's and Aiyanna's conversation earlier about sacred trees and their significance. A flush of embarrassment heated his cheeks— he'd been so distracted, he'd completely missed those vital details.

"I'm sorry, that's my fault," he said apologetically. "But wait...," his voice regaining its urgency. He counted the dots on Willow's map, then turned his back to the split rock. With bated breath, he paced out the distance towards the distant mountain range, stopping at the ridge of the cliff, just above the ledge. It wasn't an exact measurement, but the number of steps equated roughly to the number of dots. The size of a 'step' on the map was up for interpretation, but it would be in a close enough range if the steps were a bit longer or shorter.

But something far more significant dawned on him. With the split rock at his back and the missing peak still in his line of sight, the path he had just paced out led him directly to the location of the hidden ledge he had seen through the split!

A surge of adrenaline shot through him. He dropped to his knees, his gaze scrutinizing the cliff wall between the summit and the ledge they knew existed below. And there it was, etched into the rock face—the same symbol from Nanny's map, a clear confirmation that they had not only deciphered the final clue but were standing right at the entrance to the hidden path.

They had done it. Relief and triumph washed over them, erasing the doubt and frustration of just moments before.

While there were more symbols to decipher on the map, they were now confident they understood the thought process required. They decided to move on to Silas's cave.

18

LESSONS OF WAR

Over lunch, Aiyanna told Nanny about the progress she, Willow, and Kai had made earlier that morning, before they left. Nanny's interest was piqued by her story of the Ceiba tree. It was also a sacred tree in Africa; she wanted to hear more about her grandmother, and the stories she told Aiyanna.

Aiyanna recounted stories of her youth and her precious memories with her grandmother. Nanny appeared truly interested; wanting to know more about the Map of Sacred Places, its origins and the Spanish. Aiyanna told it all, just as she did with the others. With Nanny all caught up, she asked the question that had been on her mind, since Kai first mentioned Nanny's Map of Trails.

"But the thing I'm really curious about..." Aiyanna paused, a thoughtful glint in her eyes, "...is your map? Who gave it to you, Nanny? And why?"

Nanny smiled... as memories of her younger years came flooding back.

I was much younger then, filled with passion and a sense of invincibility, as only the young feel. The plan was audacious: raid the British outpost, secure their precious guns and ammunition, and vanish back into the hills without them knowing.

We were a small band, about a dozen maroons, hardened by

years of ambushes, skirmishes, and raids, and a small contingent of Taino warriors. As the years of skirmishes mushroomed to outright war, many of the Taino young men joined our cause, for it was their fight for home. This was their land, stolen from their forebears; we were brought here, but they belonged. They saw it as a fight to reclaim the land of their ancestors.

The British somehow knew we were coming and were waiting... I heard a rustle, then a barked order, and musket fire tore through the undergrowth. Planning is meaningless in situations like these, you have to trust gut instincts. We were caught unawares, nowhere to go. There was another contingent of redcoats behind us, blocking a retreat. We were encircled, outnumbered... We had no choice but to fight.

Steel clashed and we fought with the savagery of those who knew the only choice was fight or death. Machetes carved through the air, answered by the sharp crack of musket fire, and the swoosh of arrows, set in flight by our Taino brothers; whispers of death with chilling precision.

The jungle floor was washed in red. For every British soldier that fell, it seemed two more took his place. We couldn't hold forever so with a desperate cry, I rallied our forces. Desperation gave us strength. Blind determination filled us as we surged forward, choked by gunpowder and blinded by the thick smoke. Till finally we pushed them back. Limping and bleeding we fled into the shelter of the dense forest, the air heavy with the acrid smell of gunpowder.

Days later, we made it back to my village, we were battered but alive. The cheers that greeted us were quickly muted by the specter of our losses.

As the wounded were being tended to, I was pulled aside by an elderly priestess who was visiting. She was on the way to her Taino village further in the mountains. I still remember her eyes, dark and fathomless, they saw not just the survival, but the heavy price it carried.

She led me away from the sight or earshot of anyone, and reaching into a worn leather pouch slung over her shoulder, she pulled out a rolled parchment.

"This path you walked," the priestess traced the route of the ambush, "it was one of blood and needless pain. Yet, there are others..."

She unfurled the map further, showing a web of hidden trails, known to her people for generations. "We walked these like spirits," she whispered, "and could have spared you such sacrifice."

As I looked at the map, the lines forming a complex mosaic of trails, I saw its value, but it was then that I truly understood —war is not just a series of battles, but a contest of knowledge and wisdom. To know the land, its secrets, and its dangers is power. To use that knowledge wisely is how victories are truly won.

.   .   .

Having decoded the symbols, Kai and Willow ventured onto the hidden trail to Silas with a mix of exhilaration and trepidation. The treacherous narrow ledge, a path of loose rocks and uneven terrain wound, its way along the sun-baked cliff face.

The heat radiated off the exposed rock, shimmering in the air around them. The exposed trail devoid of any shade offered no respite as the unyielding rays of the sun assaulted them. Small shrubs with spindly stems and small leaves, clung to the craggy face of the cliff, stunted from a lack of moisture and the vicious glare.

Willow lifted her hand, signaling Kai to stop as they neared the cave entrance. "Wait," she whispered, her voice barely louder than the rustle of the wind.

She cupped her hands around her mouth. "Silas?" she called, her voice hushed and urgent. "It's us! It's Willow and Kai!"

The silence stretched, thick tension thickening. Willow could feel her heart thudding in her chest as she exchanged a worried glance with Kai. Had he left? Were they too late?

Then, a faint rustle from the cave's shadowy depths. A flicker of movement, barely visible in the dim light.

"Willow? Kai?" Silas's voice, raspy with disuse, cut through the silence. But fear and suspicion lingered in his tone. He'd been on the run for a week, hunted like an animal. Trust didn't come easily.

"It's us, Silas," Willow called back, her voice laced with reassurance. "We've come back."

Hesitantly, Silas emerged from the shadows, his eyes narrowed against the blinding sunlight. It took a moment for them to adjust, and as his vision cleared, the wariness faded, replaced first with surprise, then relief.

"Willow!" His voice broke, a mix of joy and disbelief. "You came back!"

As they stepped into the cool dimness of the cave, a welcome respite from the unrelenting heat outside, Kai paused briefly. He noticed the encircled symbol with the bat ears etched into the rock by the entrance. Their initial assumption was correct—the symbol represented the cave. He had missed it the first time. Willow's eyes adjusted slowly, making out Silas's form somewhere in a corner, surrounded by dried leaves and makeshift bedding.

"Are you alright?" Kai asked, his voice filled with concern as he cautiously moved closer.

Silas pushed himself up, wincing slightly. "Better," he managed, a ghost of a smile flickering across his face. "Your herbs have done wonders, Ms. Willow. The wounds have closed but it's still tender beneath, and I'm regaining my strength with each passing day."

Willow beamed. "I knew they would! Now, let me have another look..."

Sitting beside him, she gently unwrapped the bandages. The injuries, while still visible, were healing remarkably well. His skin, though still marred by rough edges of the scab that had formed, was no longer inflamed. She smiled reassuringly. "You'll be back to your old self in no time."

Silas leaned back, his face alight with a mix of relief and gratitude. "I can't thank you enough," he began, before his voice caught. "Have... have they been searching?" he asked, a tremor in his words.

Kai knelt beside him. "Yes," he confirmed gently. "The manhunt has intensified, but there are seven of us, including Nanny, working to help you." Willow also included Aiyanna's mother, Maroya, in her count of trusted collaborators.

"Nanny? She is working to help me?" Silas remained speechless, not knowing what to say. He knew of the revered fighter and leader and was surprised to hear that she was trying to help. He knew the risks she assumed by doing so. Hearing her name gave him additional resolve to succeed.

Silas nodded, a frown creasing his brow. "I know they won't give up," he murmured. "I heard them the day before yesterday. It was strange, like they were right in the cave with me..."

Willow and Kai exchanged a glance. "Tell us more," Kai urged, his mind racing.

"The voices, ...they were very muffled but echoed everywhere—as if they were coming from the ceiling. It sounded like they were on the other side of the roof."

Kai's eyes gleamed. "Silas, I believe you. We've found out a few things since we left you... more things about the cave." He hesitated for a moment, gauging Silas's reaction. "There's a lot to tell, and it might explain why you heard the men the way you did. I've been thinking... what if there are hidden tunnels in the ceiling, connecting to other caverns above us? That's the only way what you heard makes sense. And if there are more caves above us, what's to say they don't have their own exits and entrances?"

Silence hung in the air as Silas considered Kai's words, his exhaustion momentarily forgotten. "You mean... "

"Yes," Willow finished, determination shining in her eyes. "That explains why you could hear the echoes all around you. We need to find those tunnels—they could be your way out."

A spark ignited in Silas's eyes. He rose to his feet, a sense of purpose replacing his lingering fear. "Then let's get to it," he declared. "What do I need to do?"

Kai grinned, impressed by Silas's eager determination. "First, we're going to need a few things. We'll need a long sturdy branch, something we can use to probe for hollows in the ceiling. I left one on the trail outside the entrance. We'll eventually need to find a way of getting you up there when the time comes... maybe we can create a makeshift platform with some of the rocks in here.

"We've also brought some vines," Willow added. "They are at the cave entrance. We'll need to plait them together to make them stronger and tie them to make them longer. We'll go get more if we need it."

Kai looked at Silas with a smile. "We're going to tear this cave apart until we find something, Silas. I feel it in my bones.

We'll spend the night and do it again tomorrow, but I know there is an exit."

"Hallelujah, Mr. Kai." Silas laughed, his spirit lifted. "And I am so thankful, I have a night with company to look forward to, there is nothing more joyful than that."

A smile, the first in days, broke across Silas' face at the news of company, and the possibility of other exits energized him further. The path before him felt different this time. No longer a desperate flight, it felt charged with purpose, a march towards freedom. With each step as they searched, a flicker of hope ignited in Silas's eyes. Willow watched his change with silent pleasure. His strides held a newfound ease, the stiffness of his wounds giving way to a glimpse of his former strength —or what she imagined that strength to be. Her heart swelled with joy and hope alongside his. Though she had only known him for a few days and spent only a few hours with him, she felt like she was finally beginning to understand his substance, and she found herself drawn to it.

"Tell me more about your idea," Silas urged Kai, his voice rough but laced with genuine curiosity.

Kai explained his hunch about hidden tunnels and chambers, a vast network concealed within the mountain itself. Willow chimed in, recounting the map symbols and how they aligned eerily well with Kai's deductions.

They searched for hours by the flickering light of torches, fashioned from bundled twigs and branches tied together and soaked in boar fat. They scoured the walls and roof of the cave, exploring every tunnel they found. They remained undaunted, though their eyes burned and their feet ached with exhaustion. When they finally gave up the search, they agreed that it would be wisest to eat and rest, and try again the next day with fresh eyes and clearer minds.

They settled down and shared the rations they brought, the smoky scent of the dying fire mingling with the musty dampness of the cave. With a touch of hesitation, Willow spoke. "Sean wanted me to tell you something... Sarah's alright."

A flicker of surprise, then relief washed over Silas's face. "Sarah," he breathed, "thank God. I prayed every night for her. I thought she was dead when I saw her still body on the ground." Her image had plagued his mind for the duration he'd been in the cave. Confirmation that she was safe was the balm his troubled soul needed. A lightness, a sense of hope, replaced the crushing weight of worry that had burdened him since he fled.

A shared understanding passed between them. Silas's act of defiance, his desire to protect Sarah, resonated deeply with both Willow and Kai. It painted a picture of a young man with a compassionate heart, trapped in a cruel system.

19

MISGUIDED STRIKE

A hush settled across the village as twilight overcame the last rays of the sun. Milton paced the confines of his dimly lit home fuming, a whirlwind of fury inside him. Mr. Thomas's ultimatum echoed in his head. "Fail to do so, Mr. Keynes, and the consequences will be... unpleasant." What would he do if he didn't find the evidence? The unfinished threat lingered, worse than any outright declaration of what was in store for him. He'd heard of Thomas's capacity for cruelty when slighted. Desperation gnawed at him; twenty-four hours was not enough time.

Then it occurred to him, a stark reminder of his objective: Get a grip, Milton, this has nothing to do with the slave. It doesn't matter if Olu was innocent. Now is the perfect time to exact your revenge... He was transported back to the moment when he locked eyes with the Maroon who stole his future. Those eyes had burned a brand into his brain. He needed proof to implicate Olu, but that didn't mean he had to find it.

His gaze settled on the cluttered desk, a chaos that reflected his thoughts. Inspiration flashed. With trembling hands, he reached for a blank sheet of parchment and a quill, his heart a crescendoing beat against his chest. He considered himself an honorable man, and in many ways he was, but he knew what he had to do, even if it meant destroying his own honor in the process.

Milton's hand trembled as he crafted the letter: Get a hold, man, the voice within him said, this time louder. This is no time for cowardice. The words flowed thereafter, each word a meticulous lie aimed at casting Olu as a traitor. The weight of the ultimatum crushed him, but the desire to get his revenge was greater.

"Dear Olu," he began, the words infused with a false warmth he had never felt for the man. "I trust you are well." He paused, desperately seeking the words to manufacture evidence without arousing suspicion. He carefully crafted the letter, rereading it to be sure the right tone was inflected.

"Dear Olu, I trust you are well. Our plans progress smoothly, and your assistance has been invaluable. Silas's escape is imminent—your loyalty will be richly rewarded in due course."

Milton paused, a wave of guilt washing over him, but he quickly pushed it aside. His own survival depended on this deception. Sealing the completed letter with wax, Milton contemplated his next move. Presenting it to Mr. Thomas would be his final, desperate play.

He would approach Mr. Thomas, weaving a tale of suspicion and surveillance. He'd claim to have witnessed Olu exchanging messages with an unknown figure over the past days. He would describe lying in wait along the trail, confronting the mysterious contact on his way to meet Olu. A struggle ensued, the figure escaped, but not before Milton snatched the damning note.

He knew the timing was suspicious, but he'd just play dumb. He'd describe it as a gamble, a desperate one. He had no way of knowing when they'd meet again, but keeping watch was his only hope. It was risky, a shot in the dark, but it had paid off. He was ready to face the consequences if it hadn't. With his story meticulously crafted, resolve hardened within Milton. He had been forced into a corner, but he refused to surrender without a fight.

. . .

Sunlight streamed through the vertical seams of the window shutters, painting stripes across the walls. With a yawn, Sean stretched, the creak of his joints piercing the stillness of the morning. Olu's knock at his door had awoken Sean from a deep sleep.

He and Olu had gone directly to Sean's house the previous night after the meeting with the others, and stayed up until the wee hours of the morning discussing their part of the plan. They needed a foolproof way to direct the search away from Silas's hiding place and the escape route. Sean felt as if he'd only slept a couple of hours when Olu's knock startled him awake.

Olu was already at the table, poring over the map, a half-eaten piece of bread beside him, when Sean rejoined him.

"You came back early... Couldn't sleep?" Sean asked, his own eyes heavy with exhaustion.

"Too much on my mind," Olu replied, his hands fumbling clumsily as he sifted through the notes he'd scrawled the night before. "We need that fire rumor to be taken seriously. It's our best chance to draw attention away from Silas."

Sean poured himself a cup of water from the clay jug on the table, his voice low and contemplative. "The way I see it is this: there're three things that need to happen without a glitch," he began, pausing to emphasize his points. "First, the timing of the news about the campfire needs to be perfect. Second, we'll need to convince Quao to select you to lead the search without him suspecting he's being led to that decision. And third, we'll need Thomas to come with us."

He took a sip of water before continuing. "I think number three is easy if we can get one and two to work. News of a campfire in the backcountry will be the most concrete lead they've had so far. Thomas is hellbent on revenge, and he won't want to miss the opportunity to be there when Silas is found."

Olu was silent as he processed Sean's words. "I agree with that... Nanny seemed convinced Jiro would pull it off and I think Quao will select me to lead if you suggest it."

"Really? Why?" Sean asked.

A sly grin spread across his face as Olu answered. "His butt is covered, if it turns out to be a failure in any way. He can't be blamed; he responded to a believable lead, and the person selected to lead was recommended by a white settler."

Sean grinned. "His butt is covered," he agreed, impressed by Olu's plan. A sharp knock interrupted the moment. Sean and Olu exchanged a concerned look. It was still early for unplanned visitors... Sean answered the door to find Phillip standing there, an unexpected guest.

Phillip blinked in surprise, clearly not expecting Olu. A wave of apologies rushed from him. "Sean, my apologies, I didn't realize you had a guest. I can come back later..."

"Nonsense!" Sean said, stepping back to usher him in. "Come in, come in. You know you're always welcome. But... you seem troubled. What's on your mind?"

Phillip hesitated, his gaze darting between Olu and Sean. Sean sensing his conflict to continue or leave, urged him to continue.

"Phillip, it's OK to speak if it's Olu you are worried about."

He swallowed hard, as if steeling himself. "I... came because, ...well, last night, Tom and I were at the tavern and we heard..." He paused, unsure how to continue.

Sean's eyes narrowed. The light tone was replaced by something more serious. "Heard what, Phillip?" He glanced at Olu, sensing the tension in the air. "Whatever it is, you can speak freely here."

Phillip took a deep breath. "I overheard some men talking about Milton. Apparently he went to see Mr. Thomas, claiming that Olu... " he glanced at Olu, his voice faltering slightly, "...that he was helping Silas."

A wave of tension descended upon the room. The blood drained from Olu's knuckles as he gripped the edge of the table, but his expression hardened into a mask of stoicism. "Milton," he muttered. "What is he up to and why would he do that? Sean told me, he was seen snooping around my house. What does he have against me?"

Sean's eyes flashed with anger, coming to Olu's defense. "He knows better than to spread lies like this. Especially about Olu." He placed a hand on Olu's shoulder, offering silent support.

Phillip squirmed under their scrutiny. "Olu, I know you and I have always admired your integrity." he paused trying to find the right words before continuing. "I heard he stopped in the Tavern after being rebuffed by the Justice of the Peace. He went there first and told him the same story, but he was thrown out. He then stopped at the Tavern, started drinking, before deciding to go see Mr. Thomas."

Sean was visibly perturbed, "Did he give any inclination why he believed Olu is involved?"

There was another knock at the door before Phillip could respond. It was John Tomkin who immediately sensed the tension in the air. He glanced at Phillip.

"I guess, you've told them?"

Phillip nodded, as he continued answering Sean's question. "From what I heard, Milton began rambling the more he drank. It seems it's more to do with a grudge against Olu, than about Olu helping the runaway."

"What grudge?" Olu asked. "I've barely ever spoken to the man."

John spoke then, rubbing his chin thoughtfully as he looked at Olu. "As you know, I was with Phillip. The same question was on my mind most of the night." His gaze drifted to the side, a flicker of uncertainty crossing his face. "There's something I remembered about Milton... It might be important, but" he paused, clearly conflicted, "if it's not, I'm concerned it may cause more trouble."

Olu, already perplexed, was getting impatient. "Get on with it, John. He is telling people I'm helping a runaway. That is a serious accusation. Nothing you say can make it any worse."

John hesitated, glancing at Sean, who nodded his agreement to continue. "About six months after we arrived in the village, I asked Milton why he was so aloof with the villagers. He said something about the Maroons robbing him of his future as a soldier. He said his career was cut short by a Maroon that shattered the bone in his leg with a spear."

Olu's body tensed at John's words. "Do you know which battle that was?"

"Yes, a battle with Lieutenant Thicknesse's force along the Spanish River," John replied.

"I know of the battle," Olu admitted. "I heard that the British would have had the element of surprise on their side if a soldier had not done something stupid by breaking cover and crawling into the open. I also heard that the soldier was wounded."

"You were there?" Sean asked.

"No, I wasn't," Olu replied, "but my brother was. It was a

brutal battle. He returned gravely wounded; a bullet had pierced his stomach. He told me about the battle and about the soldier he wounded with his spear. He saw the soldier break cover, focused on the far banks, but strangely, he did not pay any attention to the shrubs behind him where my brother was hiding. My brother threw his spear when he saw the soldier begin to squeeze the trigger of his musket, aiming at a Maroon on the far side." Olu paused, his eyes fixed on a distant point that seemed to hold his attention. The others understood the depth of Olu's pain and refrained from interrupting.

"My brother died five days later."

"I'm sorry for your loss, Olu." John paused, before continuing. "Milton must think it was you."

Olu stared at the table, the wood grain blurring before his eyes. A mixture of emotions overwhelmed him: grief for his brother and anger, silently betrayed by a tightly clenched muscle in his jaw.

"I think he does. My brother was two years younger, but we looked very much alike."

20

PURGED BY FIRE

Willow, Aiyanna, and Kai convened in a clearing near Nanny's house to examine the map and review their progress. Aiyanna listened intently as they recounted their discoveries. A sense of wonder surged through her as the symbols on the map transformed into a language she instinctively understood. This was her birthright, the legacy of her ancestors whispering through the ages.

For the first time since her mother shared her grandmother's aspirations for her, she fully understood the weight of being the Keeper of Wisdom. She realized her grandmother had begun shaping her from a young age. Suddenly, memories of stories and shared moments with her grandmother flooded back. The more Willow and Kai spoke, the stronger her connection to her heritage felt.

Kai continued his briefing... The lower cavern proved to be a maze of dead ends and ceiling punctures, most of which were either too small or led nowhere. The breakthrough came early the next morning. The sun had not yet risen, but the hue of its rays was visible from the cave entrance—a muted glow just above the distant horizon. They quickly discovered one tunnel that stood out from the rest shortly after starting their exploration.

This tunnel spanned about twelve paces and, like the others, ended abruptly with various-sized holes peppering its ceiling.

Midway through, the ceiling gave way to a large enough hole for a person to pass through. Initially, it seemed to lead nowhere, but upon closer inspection, they found it continued at an angle, connecting to another tunnel above. The upper tunnel provided ample standing room, but its roof gradually got lower as they followed it, eventually forcing them to crawl for about four feet before reaching another, significantly larger cavern.

They spent the morning investigating the upper cavern, which was much less intricate than the one below. It formed a round chamber with relatively uniform walls, featuring three branching tunnels. One of these tunnels was shallow, ending after about five paces. The other two, however, proved to be invaluable discoveries—they both led to exits. Both were lengthy, but one was considerably shorter. The shorter tunnel emerged further up in the mountains, while the longer one went a considerable distance, eventually opening closer to the ocean.

"Were you able to decide which would be the better escape route?" Aiyanna asked.

"We're thinking the longer one might be safer," Willow responded. "It would mean less time on the main trail, plus there is another hidden path not far from where it joins the main trail. Here, see the marker? It's not far." Willow pointed to a location on the map.

"We also figured out the meaning of the symbols too," Kai added.

Aiyanna was surprised. "Really? You mean for the other hidden path?"

"Yes. You have to get off the main trail and make your way into the forest. This marker only has two symbols."

"That simplifies things." Aiyanna muttered, more to herself than the others, now fully immersed in the symbols. "This one... two lines, close together..." She followed the lines with her finger, then her brow furrowed. "Like a tree trunk, maybe? And look, they widen out..." She gestured towards the wavy lines at the base, a smile spreading across her face. "It could be a tree, those must be the roots; likely a Ceiba tree, from how far they spread outward."

Willow glanced at Kai, they were amazed at how quickly she figured that out. They had not known what the symbol meant. It wasn't until they saw the massive Ceiba tree beside the trail that they realized it was what the symbol depicted. Maybe these symbols are ingrained in her Taino roots.

"You're amazing, Aiyanna," Willow complimented. "It took us a while to figure that out. The second symbol was easier once we saw the tree. It's a waterfall; we could see it in the distance from the location of the tree. We had to get off the trail and make our way to it."

The second symbol was a wide horizontal line, with a tight cluster of vertical dashes plummeting from its center. Beneath, and to the sides of the dashed lines were irregular shapes. One large one was in front of the vertical lines, and the others were scattered outwards, like rocks tumbled by the rushing torrent.

"We got to the falls, but we were stumped," Willow continued, then Kai figured it out.

Kai explained what happened. "We were baffled at first by the large shape in the middle, resembling a poorly drawn circle. It was missing, there was nothing large in front of the waterfall. We thought maybe it was washed away over time by erosion caused by the waterfall. But then it hit me! Remember that clue in Silas's cave—the drawing of the mountains, with one peak missing? That missing peak caused us to search for which one was missing, and that led us to focus on a specific direction. Suddenly, I realized the big boulder might not have been there all along. It was opposite to the mountains. They used something that was missing to point us in the right direction and now they are showing something that isn't really there for the same reason. Maybe it was put there to be like a message, telling us to start searching somewhere around there!"

"And he was right," Willow beamed, smiling proudly at Kai. "The entrance is behind the waterfall."

"Did you explore it?" Aiyanna asked.

"There wasn't time," Kai responded, "but I did see it; it has the matching symbols etched into its wall."

"This is where we have some questions, Aiyanna." Willow leaned over the Map of Sacred Places and pointed at a spot on the map.

"This spot marks the trailhead behind the waterfall, leading to this area here, with these drawings of flames." Willow traced her finger over an icon on the map—a cluster of flames. "This place is the only one of its kind on the entire map... Why flames here?" she whispered, her voice barely audible. "And what does this place even mean?"

Aiyanna, her features a blend of Taino and Maroon, felt a shiver run down her spine as ancient memories of a time with her grandmother, stirred within her.

"My grandmother..." Her voice cracked, the weight of generations catching in her throat.

"She told me... that hundreds of years ago, maybe even thousands, my people set forth to the sea in search of new lands. Atabey, the Goddess and Mother of all Creation, instructed Guabencex, mother of storms, volcanoes, and earthquakes, to go ahead and find and sanctify a place for the arrival of her people. Guabencex, with the might of a hurricane, went ahead and found one of the most beautiful islands she had ever seen.

She followed the land towards the rising sun and commanded it to purge itself, in preparation for her people. A sacrifice needed to be made, so a small portion of the land was offered to sanctify the whole. The beauty of the island would be preserved, but a piece of it would be forever changed, a vessel of cleansing for those seeking rebirth."

"The earth groaned," she continued, her voice trembling with the weight of ancient power. "The heart of the island cracked open, as fire shot towards the very heavens."

Willow shivered, her imagination vividly painting the once-green land transformed into a fiery inferno. Kai leaned forward, his warrior's spirit captivated by the raw power of the tale.

"The fire didn't fall like rain," Aiyanna whispered, her eyes reflecting the flickering flames of memory. "It flowed like rivers of liquid sun, burning everything, cleansing everything. The sand itself, once kissed by the sea, blackened and hardened, a testament to the island's sacrifice."

She closed her eyes, feeling the weight of untold centuries pressing down upon her. "Atabey, who was everywhere, watched and was pleased. She called upon Yucahu, spirit of the sea and cassava, to bring forth rains that cooled the molten earth. And when the land finally rested, a new place was born

—scarred, sacred, and waiting. She called it Xaymaca; land of wood and water. Atabey then commanded that this place, the place that offered up the flames, become a permanent refuge for only the purest of heart, those seeking rebirth. As the legend goes, anyone who ventures there with evil in their heart is immediately consumed by fire."

A tremor went through the group, not of fear, but of awe mixed with a spark of something dangerous and thrilling. The map before them seemed alive, its lines not just paths, but the veins of the island itself, humming with a power they were just beginning to understand.

Kai, broke the silence. "So this place here," pointing to the map, "is the place where fire erupted from the land and destroyed everything around it?"

Aiyanna nodded, her gaze distant as she remembered the ancient tales passed down through generations. "It is the most Sacred of Sacred places on the island."

"And the goddess proclaimed it a refuge for those seeking rebirth."

Again Aiyanna nodded, her thoughts drifting to the significance of the sacred sanctuary. "Yes, and those with an evil heart will be immediately consumed with fire."

"Well then, I believe this cause to be just and pure, and I don't think any of us, especially Silas, has an evil heart. That's where we should take him." With that, Kai stopped, scanning both Willow's and Aiyanna's faces. Neither spoke, but the unspoken agreement hung heavy in the air, a silent acknowledgment of the path ahead. As they contemplated their next steps, the gravity of their decision regarding Silas's fate weighed heavily on their minds, guiding them towards their shared destiny.

21

BEFORE FIRST LIGHT

A knot tightened in Olu's chest as he clenched his fist, his mind swirling with conflicting thoughts.

"This is a mess. Milton thinks I ended his career." he muttered. "Maybe the best move is just to confront him. Should I go to him, tell him it was my brother? I don't believe he knows anything about Silas or what we're doing; he's making it all up to get revenge."

Sean chewed his lip as Olu went on. "Let's map out the pros and cons first," he suggested. "We need to approach this strategically."

Olu paused, trying to rein in his temper. "OK, but be honest. What are the downsides?"

Sean hesitated. "If you confront Milton directly, there's a chance he won't believe you. Worse, he might get even more riled up. We can't predict how he'll react, and that could complicate things with Silas."

Olu's frustration grew as he absorbed Sean's words. "But I would tell him it was my brother who is now dead, that threw the spear. That's verifiable by anyone in the village. Why would he keep holding a grudge?"

Sean rubbed his chin thoughtfully. "You might be right, Olu. It could diffuse the situation. But there's still a chance that Milton's too blinded by anger to listen. We also need to consider how this affects our plans for Silas. If Milton becomes hostile, it could draw unwanted attention our way."

Olu nodded in agreement. "You have a point. We can't risk jeopardizing Silas's escape. Let's focus on that for now. We'll deal with Milton later, once we know how his actions might impact our plans."

Sean nodded in agreement. "Agreed. Our priority is Silas. Let's stay focused on what's most important."

A sudden commotion outside interrupted their conversation, drawing their attention. "It's riders." someone shouted.

"What could that be?" Sean muttered, his brow furrowed with concern.

Olu shrugged, his expression troubled. "I don't know, but it doesn't feel right."

They stepped outside and saw Mr. Thomas and another man riding into the village. Dread washed over them, this was an unexpected visit and could only mean bad news. Their minds raced with possibilities, wondering if Silas had been found or if something else had gone wrong.

Before they could make sense of the situation, Quao emerged from his hut and approached the newcomers. Sean and Olu moved closer, hoping to eavesdrop on the conversation, but the distance made it difficult to hear.

Quao briefly exchanged words with the men, before he turned back towards the village, beckoning Sean, Olu and two elders from the council, to join them. With a sinking feeling in their stomachs, they hurried over to Quao's side, bracing themselves for whatever news Thomas had brought.

"You need to hear this." Quao turned to the militia man. "Go on."

"There's been a development in the search for the runaway," the man said.

A knot formed in Sean's stomach. He glanced over, seeing his own apprehension reflected in the tense lines of Olu's face.

"We received word of a campfire in the backcountry. We believe it's a credible lead... could be the break we need," the man finished.

Sean and Olu exchanged a look of relief mingled with confusion. This wasn't part of the plan. Nanny intended for Jiro to bring news of the campfire, steering the search away. Instead, an unknown factor had forced their hand. Was this

Nanny's doing?

"Where was the campfire found?" Sean asked.

"I understand it's in an old village, further up the mountain, Sir." replied the militia man. Sean's mind raced. The same plan, just expedited... Nanny's hand must be behind this.

Thomas addressed Quao, his voice tight with urgency. "I need your help, Quao. We are headed out tomorrow at first light to investigate it. You have to find someone to lead the expedition."

Quao's eyes widened. Surprised and annoyed by the request and the way it was asked. You have to find? The audacity of the man commanding me, he thought...

"Why, Sir? You already have several of my men tracking the runaway. Surely you have capable men of your own."

Thomas's jaw clenched, a flicker of annoyance crossing his features. "They are all out on the trail and this is no ordinary expedition, Quao. This is in the backcountry. No one knows the area better than your lot. I need someone I can trust, someone who knows these lands. And I need them ready to leave at first light."

Quao's brow furrowed in thought as he considered Thomas's request. The urgency in Thomas's voice and the gravity of the situation were evident, and Quao knew they could not afford to ignore this request.

"I understand, Sir," Quao replied, his voice measured. "I'll find someone. We cannot waste any time."

Thomas nodded, his expression grave. "Thank you, Quao. We leave at first light. Meet in town, in front of the tavern."

Quao agreed with a solemn nod.

Thomas nodded in return, and as he turned to leave, his gaze fell upon Milton, standing apart in the shadows cast by the eaves of a hut. Their eyes locked, a silent exchange passing between them. Thomas's eyes narrowed, suspicion darkening his face. Milton shifted, his eyes flashing with concern beneath the bravado.

A wave of unease washed over Milton as Thomas finally looked away. He could only hear snippets, but it was enough to understand they found a lead, a campfire. It must be a good one if they came all the way to the village to get more help. The campfire intensified the risk—he was glad he hadn't delivered the forged letter yet. Even if the lead panned out, he wasn't sure that would save him from Thomas's unpredictable wrath.

Meanwhile, a seed of suspicion lodged in Thomas's mind as he rode away. Milton's isolation, that flicker of anxiety... there was more to the former soldier than met the eye. There were hidden motives buried beneath the surface. He would find them if the campfire lead did not succeed, or maybe even if it did.

The tension in the air was palpable as Thomas rode away. The villagers were left to grapple with the weight of the news. Sean exchanged a worried glance with Olu, both understanding the gravity of the situation. The unexpected turn of events left them with more questions than answers.

Quao turned to the gathered villagers, his expression grave. "We have a task ahead of us, let's see if we can make a quick job of this," he announced. "Mr. Thomas has requested our help, and we cannot afford to fail. I need volunteers to join the search tomorrow, at first light."

However, the call for volunteers met with silence. One by one, the villagers began to peter out, their apprehension evident in their hesitant movements. Quao's frustration simmered beneath the surface as he watched them disperse, muttering under his breath about Thomas's audacity.

Sean saw his opportunity to approach him as the villagers began to leave. Quao was visibly frustrated, a scowl darkening his face, as he fell into step beside him. "It's frustrating when others fail to appreciate the efforts we've already made," he remarked casually, hoping to resonate with Quao's sentiments.

Quao glanced at Sean, his brow furrowed in agreement. He scoffed in reply, shaking his head in annoyance. "But what choice do we have? Mr. Thomas is determined to find Silas, and we cannot afford to refuse his request."

Sean nodded in understanding, carefully choosing his next words. "True, but I think there's a way to ensure that this expedition is successful," he suggested. "There are still some capable men left that know the backcountry well. We can approach them one on one. We only need one."

Quao paused, considering Sean's words. "You may have a point," he conceded, narrowing his eyes slightly as he gave thought to Sean's proposal. "But who do you have in mind?"

Sean hesitated for a moment, as if weighing his options. "Let me think about it, but first, let's check what the others think," he finally responded, nodding towards the two elders who remained nearby.

With Quao's agreement, they gathered the elders for a brief meeting. As they deliberated over who should lead the expedition, one of the elders, a venerable figure known for his wisdom, brought up Olu's name.

"Yes, Olu would indeed be an excellent choice. In fact, that would have been my first choice as well," Sean affirmed, his tone matter-of-fact. "I didn't suggest him because it would require a lot of convincing. He has strong feelings that Mr. Thomas is taking advantage of us."

"He is not wrong there," Quao muttered under his breath.

Sean paused, his expression growing more serious. "Quao has bent backwards cooperating, sending our best warriors. But Mr. Thomas keeps coming back for more. Olu believes he has placed Quao in a tough position, without even a token of thanks or recognition for what Quao is doing."

"I can approach him if you want me to," Sean offered, his voice carrying a hint of confidence. "I may be able to convince him. He is a reasonable man."

Quao and the elders exchanged thoughtful looks, considering Sean's proposal. After a moment of silence, Quao nodded in agreement. "Very well," he said. "Yes, please speak with him," Quao agreed, nodding firmly. "I agree he's the right candidate. Let us know as soon as possible what he decides."

With their decision made, Sean left and met with Olu, under a large cedar tree at the edge of the village.

Sean nodded to Olu as he approached. "It's done. You'll be leading Thomas's team."

"Good," Olu replied. "I'll get with Quao later to finalize the arrangements and get any additional instructions he may have."

Nodding, Sean squeezed Olu's shoulder reassuringly. "Now the plan begins, my friend. Be careful. We don't know what Milton has been saying to Thomas about you," he paused, looking Olu in the eyes. "I'll let Quao know you've agreed. I had planned to go to Nanny Town today, but with all these changes, I think I'd better stick around. Just in case Quao changes his mind or something else comes up, I'll go tomorrow. This is so unexpected. It's all moving so quickly. My head's spinning."

Olu rubbed his temple, his lips pursed, brow furrowed. The sudden change of plans left him feeling off-kilter. "I sure hope they are ready to move Silas," he muttered more to himself.

. . .

Milton's suspicion festered, a knot in his stomach as he observed Sean and Olu. Thomas's sudden arrival and the news he brought had shattered Milton's plans. Where was Aiyanna? She had been suspiciously absent. His mind raced, the certainty settling over him: they were all colluding with sympathizers in Nanny Town to aid the runaway slave.

His attention shifted as Sean approached Quao. Even from a distance, Milton saw the tension melt from Quao's face. Whatever Sean had whispered brought the other man obvious relief. Was Quao part of it, another traitor?

He had to know. His only option was to shadow Sean closely, monitor his every action now that Olu would be accompanying Mr. Thomas. The thought of joining the party leaving in the morning briefly crossed his mind, but the memory of Thomas's stern glare was a stark warning. No, he'd stay here, watching in the shadows, unraveling their secrets piece by agonizing piece.

22

FATE'S FIRST MOVE

The air around the small group gathered at the meeting point in front of the tavern, crackled with a mix of anticipation and grim resolve. The morning mist, rolling in from the sea, enveloped them, adding an eerie atmosphere to the proceedings. Olu stood among them, his expression determined, focused on the mission ahead; hoping Kai and the others achieved success moving Silas, without any problems. Sean had met with him before he left, to confirm Olu's best estimate for timing, so he and the others could coordinate their own movements accordingly.

Quao approached Olu with Mr. Thomas beside him, "This is Olu, he will be leading you."

Thomas extended a hand in greeting. "Good to meet you, Olu. I appreciate your help." He recognized the name. Confusion clouded his thoughts, is he the one Milton mentioned? Why would Quao have chosen him if he's not trustworthy? Is Quao up to no good, or is Olu an innocent caught up in Milton's lie.

Olu gripped his hand firmly and shook it. "Good to meet you too, Sir." he replied, looking directly into Thomas's eyes. He was taken aback by its warmth. He had a very friendly and amicable demeanor; a different person from the one that rode into the village the previous day.

Quao, had had enough. He had done his part. He said his

goodbyes to Thomas and Olu, wishing them success with practiced civility. A flicker of resentment crossed his face as he glanced back at Thomas as he left.

The party consisted of five men in the group; Thomas, Spud —the militia man who had accompanied Thomas to the village, Olu and two other men, both professional slave hunters in it for a split of the bounty, or a per diem payment.

"OK men, gather around." Thomas shouted, "Spud will outline the plan for the day."

Spud addressed the men. "Today, we are headed into unfamiliar territory way up in the mountains, it will likely be difficult and dangerous. Olu here, will guide us. Hes knows the mountains well."

The men glanced over Olu, one shouted a greeting, the other giving a single nod in acknowledgement.

"We are investigating a campfire in an old abandoned village. I think this is our most credible lead so far. We believe that's where the runaway is hiding, or stopped before moving on. It's a big area so we need all the help we can get. Three other search parties will join us. We'll meet up with them in the Rio Grande valley, and travel the rest of the way as a group. The parties will split up to search the surrounding area when we reach the village. Are there any questions?"

"How long a ride is it?" one of the hunters asked.

"It will take most of the day," Olu replied.

"OK then," Spud shouted. "Let's mount up.

A sense of unease remained with Thomas as the men did their final checks. He had pieces of the puzzle but the picture remained incomplete. Glancing at Olu, he searched for any sign of deception or guilt in the man's demeanor. But Olu's expression revealed nothing, his features a mask of stoicism.

Part of him wanted to confront Olu, to demand answers and unravel the truth once and for all. But another part hesitated, wary of tipping his hand too soon. If Milton's accusations are true, Olu could be dangerous.

I'll play along, for now, he resolved, his gaze never leaving Olu's face. But I'll be watching closely, and if Olu steps out of line..."

With a terse nod, the team began the journey. Thomas fell into step behind Olu, his mind ablaze with conflicting thoughts and simmering distrust.

. . .

Milton rose before dawn to see them leave. He watched Sean approach Olu, the two exchanging quiet words in the misty half-light. Joined soon after by Quao, his arrival breaking the hushed conversation. After a brief exchange, Olu and Quao departed, and Sean turned and re-entered his home. It was now mid-morning, and Sean still had not emerged.

Milton seethed with frustration and anxiety. He'd gone into town the previous day to find Chicken, his usual henchman, but had no luck. He'd left word with the bartender for Chicken to find him if he turned up.

Just then, he saw Sean leave with a bag over his shoulder, heading toward the trail. He suspected this would happen. Chicken had told him Kai had gone to Nanny Town, the day he trailed him, and he was convinced that was Sean's destination as well. His gut told him Nanny Town was the heart of the conspiracy. It was a long walk and would be painful with his old injury, but with Chicken nowhere to be found, he had to execute his backup plan.

He was so convinced of Sean's destination—Nanny Town, the place he now believed was the nexus of their treachery—that he'd give him a head start, then leave on horseback an hour or so later.

He couldn't enter the village—that would be stupid—but he would watch from the fringes, hoping to see Sean and who he met, and he would stay as long as was necessary.

There was still no word from Chicken, so Milton left on horseback about ninety minutes after Sean. Deliberately choosing a different route to avoid accidentally crossing paths with Sean on his way to Nanny Town, he tied his horse to a young tree some distance from the village, fairly confident that by now Sean would have arrived ahead of him at the village.

After securing his horse, Milton walked back towards the village, scouting for the best vantage point. He settled into a secluded spot to observe the village's activities. Nanny's house stood in a small clearing, directly within his line of sight yet secluded from the main settlement. It was strategically backed against a dense wall of trees and thick underbrush for added security.

Hours passed, and the day wore on without activity. The afternoon sun beat down relentlessly, and the buzzing of insects seemed to grow louder with each passing moment. Sweat trickled down Milton's brow as he shifted uncomfortably in his hiding spot. Another hour, maybe two, had slipped away, and still no sign of activity. A flicker of doubt gnawed at him. Was he wrong about Sean? About Nanny Town? He stifled a yawn, exhaustion threatening to overtake him. Yet, a stubborn determination remained. The sun began its final descent, casting long shadows as the day's relentless heat finally began to ease. The village fell silent, broken only by the insistent peeping of frogs and the chirping of crickets, as the light succumbed to the creeping darkness. Resignation crept into his thoughts. Perhaps it was time to admit defeat, retreat, and regroup. With a sigh, Milton started to rise, ready to slink back to where his horse was tethered...

Just as he began his retreat, a movement caught his eye. Sean and Aiyanna emerged from Nanny's house, followed by Kai. After exchanging a few words with a girl inside, they turned towards another dwelling nearby, the door closing behind them. The coincidence was too stark to ignore. Milton's instincts sparked; he was onto something big.

With all thoughts of leaving dispelled, he hunkered down. He waited until it was evident everyone was in for the night before going back to the place where he had left his horse. He had packed some provisions. It was a last-minute decision. Now he was glad that he did. Deciding against a fire, he ate some bread and water, then slept.

.   .   .

Sean had spotted Milton in the distance as he departed Crawford Town. Aware that Milton had seen him leave, he briefly considered the possibility of Milton following but dismissed it due to Milton's bad leg; he wouldn't have been able to keep up.

Upon his arrival at Nanny Town, Sean went straight to Nanny's house, confident he wasn't followed. Willow answered the door, and they were all there: Willow, Aiyanna, Kai, and Nanny. After exchanging greetings, he dived into the question most pressing to him: How was the progress of their plans for Silas?

They quickly brought him up to speed on their success in deciphering the code, and their learned understanding of how to view and interpret the symbols. They described the secret passages that they had found in Silas's cave, and most important, their exits. Sean was relieved by their progress.

"That is fantastic progress. The timing couldn't be more perfect," he said, informing them about Mr. Thomas's visit to the village and Olu's appointment as leader. "They left at dawn this morning. I'm so sorry I wasn't here yesterday like we planned. I felt I should stay and see them off in case anything changed, but now we have to hurry. There's not much time left."

Their response was more muted than he expected. They clearly knew more than he did. Turning to Nanny, he asked, "Was that your doing?"

Nanny's gaze remained unwavering as she reclined in her crude chair, fingers steepled against her lips. She deliberated before responding cryptically, "Silas's journey began with Willow. It seems to have chosen her to share its secrets."

Sean looked at Aiyanna, puzzled. There was no help there. He looked back at Nanny and admitted apologetically, "I'm sorry, Nanny, but I don't understand."

"It's not 'my doing'," she clarified, "but I facilitated. I interpreted a message meant for Willow, who isn't yet equipped to understand it. I simply set things in motion."

"I see," he said, though he wasn't entirely sure he did. He could tell that the others still knew more than he did.

Sean saw Kai glance at Willow, an unspoken question in his stare, and Willow's imperceptible agreement.

"Sean," Kai began. "Willow has been having some dreams. She had one the night we spent with Silas. Nanny believes it means Olu is in immediate danger, and it was a message to act quickly."

Aiyanna picked up the story. "We couldn't get word to you of the change. We were afraid the plan to have Jiro bring the message of the campfire to Quao may have taken too long. We were worried Quao may not take it seriously enough to act quickly. So Nanny found another way to get the message directly to Mr. Thomas. We knew Quao would take it more seriously if it came directly from Mr. Thomas."

"And, we know he hates Silas and wants revenge." Willow finished. "There is no way Mr. Thomas could resist following up, or not being there when Silas is found."

"What was the dream?" Sean asked.

Willow glanced at Nanny, who remained silent, then at the others. They were all looking at her. It was her decision what happened next.

"It was the night before we found the tunnels," she started, pausing to collect herself. "We'd scoured every inch with no luck, so we decided to pick it up again early the next morning. In the dream..."

"I am trapped. In a dark suffocating ravine with Kai, Silas, and Kai's uncle. I don't know how I knew he was Kai's uncle; it was strange, I knew I'd never met him, but I also knew who he was. Something is hunting us, I never figured out what it was, but it is hunting us, our lives are in danger, and our only way out is blocked. My heart was beating like a hammer, pounding with panic as we desperately searched for another way out.

Suddenly, the uncle runs towards us, his face twisted in fear. 'No time! Move!' he shouts. Silas's face immediately transforms at his shout, it becomes the face of a cornered warrior determined to face his death. He turns to me and commands, 'Go! Take Kai with you. I'll stay. I'll protect you— if they come; run, don't stop and don't look back.' We locked eyes, his, filled with determination. 'You hear me?' he growled, 'Run! Save yourselves.'

My tears welled up, stinging my eyes. We can't leave him! Then, as if through a mist, a hidden crevice appeared in the ravine wall, behind thick vines. Hope surges within me, and I seize Silas's hand, but Silas hesitates. I grabbed his hand. 'We fight together, or not at all!' I said.

He looked at me, then at Kai, and something in his eyes softened. We made our way through the narrow passage. We heard a battle raging behind us and looked back; the uncle wasn't there. He had stayed to fight whatever was chasing us. The passage opened onto a path, and just as we stepped forward, a flash of slithering scales vanished into the bushes. A hissing whisper seemed to linger on the wind."

The room was silent, Sean was speechless. Finally, he

spoke.

"Oh man, that was some dream." He remained lost in thought a while longer, eyes fixed on something that was not there. "That was something," he said again.

Pulling himself back to the moment, he asked, "Have we decided where we're taking Silas, and how to get there?"

"Yes we have," Kai replied, "but it's getting late and it's a long story. We should go. I'll fill you in, then we can discuss together as a group in the morning."

"You're right, we should get some rest. We have a lot to do tomorrow." With that, Sean stood up.

Nanny also rose to her feet. "You, Aiyanna and Kai will spend the night at a house not far from here. Kai knows where."

They said their farewells, exiting Nanny's hut for the place they would spend the night. Their exit was ill-timed: Had they lingered just a few minutes longer, the course of events would have unfolded quite differently. Unbeknownst to them, Milton saw them leave. Their departure had caught his attention at the very moment he was about to abandon his mission. Little did they realize, their timing in leaving was to become the catalyst for a chain of unfortunate events.

23

TRAIL OF DECEPTION

Olu awoke to the bitter March cold of the Blue Mountains, his body stiff from a restless night. He watched them sleep, oblivious to his deception. Today, they would begin their climb, following a trail that promised discovery but led only to disappointment. Images of the previous day—the arrival of reinforcements, Thomas's palpable distrust—filled his mind. Something had to change. He couldn't let suspicion derail his plans.

Now, as the first rays of dawn painted the sky, Olu stifled a yawn, his bones aching from the relentless search and sleepless night. The search party stirred, preparing for the arduous day ahead.

Spud approached, seeking an overview of the plan. "Good morning," he greeted, forging ahead without waiting for a reply. "What do you suggest we do today? Finding the campfire was promising but disappointing; clearly a few days old. But what about the other clues?"

Olu gestured towards the towering range above them, its peak outlined sharply against the brightening sky. "Based on the clues your men found, we should head up there. That's about 2,800 feet in approximately a mile from our current position, with steep and loose rocks. We'll need to follow the ridgeline for a three-mile uphill climb to approximately 6,900 feet. That has to be completed today if we want to reach the peak tomorrow, a little more than 7,400 feet."

He paused, letting the magnitude of the task sink in. "We need to cover the entire ridgeline, the most likely route he took, as well as each side. We'll decide the next steps based on what we find."

Spud nodded, then turned to the men. "OK men, listen up, we have a long day ahead of us. We split into three teams: ridge and two flanks. Ridge team, that's the most likely route he took, so keep your eyes peeled for signs. Flanks, scour those slopes, every inch. Don't take your eyes off the ground."

Turning to Olu, he asked, "Do you have anything to add, Olu? Anything we should be aware of?"

"This journey isn't for the faint of heart," Olu said, his voice steady. "The terrain is unforgiving, and the conditions and the weather can turn on you in an instant. We need to be prepared for anything these mountains can throw at us. It'll be slow going, and dangerous." He emphasized the risks without exaggeration, making sure they understood the difficulty, but not painting an unnecessarily bleak picture.

He held their gaze, searching for the cracks he knew were there. A flicker of unease crossed a manhunter's face, followed by another. Whispers crackled through the group, barely audible at first, then growing bolder. Spud's jaw clenched, the lines of his sun-weathered face tightening with unspoken concern.

"This isn't worth it," a lone voice from the back cut through the murmurs. Not one of the younger recruits, Olu observed, but a seasoned tracker. "The reward isn't big enough to risk my life. I'm turning back, anyone else?"

A grizzled veteran stepped forward, his weathered face set in grim determination. "Count me in, Olu. We came to catch a man, didn't we? The rest of you can go weep to your mamas!"

A ripple of uncertainty washed over those still undecided. Then, one, and then another one, raised their hand, shame and defiance warring across their faces. The others watched, a mixture of resentment and lingering doubt clouding their eyes.

Spud exploded then, his gruffness amplified by contempt. "Fine, leave then, you good-for-nothing cowards!" His words lashed out, each one landing like the crack of a whip.

Altogether, four left, the full contingent of one of the search parties that had joined them the day before.

The departing men turned their backs without a farewell, leaving a chasm of doubt and strained camaraderie in their wake.

Olu assessed his diminished force, his stomach knotting. Resolute, yes, but painfully fewer. Wavering; some, but not all. Four men gone, and with them an increased risk to those helping Silas. He had to keep the rest committed to the search, to buy time for the others to move Silas. His task was a delicate balance—mentally preparing the men for what was ahead, without scaring them off prematurely.

Spud made the call to mount, and the party began their advance. Olu took the lead, and Thomas pulled his horse up beside him.

"Looks like we have some serious riding ahead," Thomas began, his tone light and conversational. "How did you come to know these lands so well?"

Olu glanced sideways at Thomas, his features relaxed but guarded. "I was born and raised in the village," he replied, his voice steady. "I spent my whole life exploring these mountains, hunting, and learning the lay of the land."

Thomas nodded, feigning interest as he probed further. "Impressive. How did you end up with the unenviable task of leading this expedition? Quite the responsibility."

A hint of pride flickered in Olu's eyes as he spoke. "Quao asked me," he explained simply. "He knows my capabilities." A thought occurred to him at that moment: Playing this cat and mouse game was pointless, best to tackle it head-on.

"Look," he said, "some friends told me yesterday that they heard some tavern gossip that Milton has been telling you things... about me. So I understand why you would be suspicious. Why don't you just ask?"

Thomas was taken aback by Olu's question, but he was impressed by his directness. The man rose a couple of notches in his esteem; his fearless advance deserved an equally direct response.

"Yes, he did approach me. He said you are aiding Silas. Are you?"

Olu turned in his saddle and looked directly in Thomas's eyes. "Sir, thank you for being honest. I also heard, what you may not have heard, that Milton blames me for an injury that ended his career as a soldier. An injury he sustained in a battle that I was not present in, and that is easily verifiable. I had intended to approach him directly, but then you rode in, and this assignment took precedence. I'll tell you what I will tell him when I get the chance to: I do know of the battle and how he was injured. I was told this by the person who inflicted his injury, my brother, who died five days after that battle from injuries he received during that battle. Now, clearly Milton is motivated by some grudge, but it's wrongly placed. I don't expect you to believe me without proof, but I do ask that you verify this on your return. Ask as many people as you need to satisfy your doubts. In the meantime, I'll lead this search as best I can, knowing I've been upfront with you."

Thomas remained impassive, his features giving nothing away. "I appreciate your candor, Olu," he replied finally, his voice neutral. "I'll consider your words carefully. Now, we have a mountain to climb."

Olu watched as Thomas disengaged, reining in his horse sufficiently for Olu to take the lead. He knew he had struck a chord. He hadn't broken Thomas, and hadn't necessarily earned his trust. However, he had complicated the game. The accusations simmering beneath the surface now had a counterpoint, a truth easily verifiable. The weight of suspicion now shifted, ever so slightly, towards Milton.

With a newfound sense of control, Olu straightened his spine. Now, it was Thomas's turn. The climb loomed, a daunting challenge, but one he was prepared to face. The path ahead might be treacherous, but he had taken the first step, playing his hand with calculated risk.

· · ·

Milton lurked in the fringes, hidden by the dense foliage... watching.

There was a chill in the air, the sky a deep indigo laced with the fading remnants of the last few stars. He could see through a narrow gap between the trees, the undulating contours of the distant mountain range taking shape as the darkness faded: a silhouette against the fading backdrop. A faint breeze carried the scent of damp earth and the rustle of unseen creatures adjusting to the coming day.

He settled back into his vigil, the same perch he'd left last night. The sun had not yet risen, but the night was receding. That was when he saw the girl from last night, leave Nanny's house. No one leaves their house at this hour without a compelling cause, he thought. That must be Nanny's daughter, he realized. That must be her. He watched her approach the house Sean, Aiyanna and Kai had entered the previous night. She knocked, Kai opened the door, and she entered.

Was this the break he'd sought? Silas, the fugitive... if he could deliver him, the whispers about his failed charge would finally fade. He needed this to work. One slip, and years of clawing back respect could vanish, just like that reckless rush on the riverbank.

He had to know what was going on inside. But how could he get closer without risking exposure?

A plan sparked in his mind. The dense wall of foliage shielding the back of Nanny's house—a tangle of vines and leaves almost impenetrable—thinned as it curved southward. Here, trees grew sparser, edging along the side of his target house... perhaps fifteen feet away. Scrawny underbrush offered scant cover, but it was better than his current vantage. If he moved over there, he might snatch scraps of conversation, or a glimpse through a window...

He scrambled back to his horse, skirting the village. Dismounting, he tied the animal and tore into the woods on foot. Had he judged the distance right? A wave of relief washed over him, his tense shoulders slumping as the treeline loomed ahead. He'd overshot the mark, recognizing his earlier hiding spot across the clearing. A swift adjustment, and finally, his target house came into view. He crept closer.

Inside the house, the group gathered over the maps as they discussed the route they would use to extract Silas to safety.

"See here," Kai said, pointing to a location on the map. "This is where the tunnel we'll take, exits."

"That one is in the north towards the sea," Sean observed. "This one heads south, to the mountain where I thought we'd take him. It's shorter, so riskier; it's more time on the main trails, but it goes towards the mountain."

"It does," Willow agreed. "But there is a good reason for going north. Aiyanna, tell him the story you told us."

Aiyanna shifted Sean's focus to the map of sacred places. "See this cluster of flames? It is one of a kind on the entire map, and for good reason. It is considered by my people to be the most Sacred of Sacred places."

She paused as she gathered her thoughts, memories of her grandmother flooding back. She recounted the story she told Kai and Willow. The story of Atabey, and Guabencex, who wielded the power of the earth's fury. How they prepared the island for the arrival of her people, the Tainos. How Guabencex searched until she found one of the most beautiful islands she had ever seen. How she chose this spot as an offering of sacrifice to sanctify the whole island. She told of the fire—a cleansing inferno that roared from the earth and the rivers of molten flame that flowed, scarring the land, turning the sand black as they reached the sea.

Sean listened in silence, the unfamiliar names and vivid imagery holding his attention. Returning to the map of trails, Aiyanna pointed to the same location Kai had.

"This is where the tunnel from Silas's cave exits, now follow the line to here." Her finger traced across the map to another point. "See these symbols? They match those at the hidden trailhead leading to the place of flames."

He glanced at the map of trails, then back to the sacred places, his eyes flicking between the marked locations Aiyanna had described.

He nodded, his eyes squinted and lips pursed. "I see that, but why here and not in the mountains?"

Willow gave Aiyanna a glance that held a shared understanding. "Aiyanna's grandmother said that the gods commanded the place where the flames erupted to be a permanent refuge... for rebirth, and for the purest of heart."

"It is believed," Aiyanna continued, catching Willow's glance and offering a slight nod, "that any who enter tainted with evil will be consumed by sacred fire."

"I believe this is the perfect place to take Silas," Kai concluded.

Things began to click for Sean. Seemingly unrelated fragments of knowledge and memories shuffled into place. His eyes widened slightly, a flicker of realization crossing his face before he schooled his features.

Pointing towards the cluster of flames on the map, he said, "Kai, I think you are right. This is the perfect area. The sand is black in the surrounding areas like Hope Bay. Some among the British avoid the area, a large region they call the Black Hills. The more superstitious think it brings bad luck or is haunted... don't know why, but they do. That may very well be the perfect spot for someone to live a life hidden in plain sight."

A murmur of agreement rippled through the group. The decision was made. Kai nodded solemnly, a determined glint in his eyes. "Willow and I need to leave as soon as possible," he stated firmly. "Silas needs to be at his new sanctuary before the search party in the mountains return. We have two, maybe three days at max, if they go all the way, but if they give up and turn back, that could be in as little as a day."

Meanwhile, outside the house, Milton lurked in his hiding place, edged with frustration. The cowitch still itched like wildfire, a maddening distraction he willed himself to ignore. The rising sun had driven him deeper into the shadows, where he carelessly brushed against the stinging nettle, causing severe itching and stinging. Now, he couldn't get close enough. He could see figures moving inside, their voices a muffled hum. Every so often, a word cut through—Silas... Black Hills... Hope Bay. His suspicion hardened into certainty. The mention of the name, 'Silas', was enough confirmation for him. They were aiding the runaway.

24

GRASPING AT STRAWS

Milton's mind swirled with obsessive determination, the overheard snippets of conversation weaving a flimsy map: Silas... Black Hills... Hope Bay... He rubbed his bad leg, a habit he'd developed whenever stress gripped him, the pain serving as a relentless reminder of his physical limitations.

Following them on foot was impossible; his horse's hooves would announce his presence long before he could catch sight of them. Panic bubbled to the surface, but he forcefully suppressed it. Time was not his friend, and wallowing in self-pity would gain him nothing.

Desperation ignited a spark in his mind. He'd gamble on the scraps of information he had gathered and stake his meager chance on his knowledge of the area. The Black Hills area wasn't small, but he could narrow down the likely trails. If he camped out and moved strategically, he might—just might—intercept the fugitives. It was a long shot, his last shot, and he was going to take it.

He contemplated heading to the tavern to drum up some help. It wouldn't be too far out of his way; the road passed by the tavern on the route to Hope Bay. Instead of continuing straight along the coastline, it turned inland, skirting the edges of the Black Hills. Most avoided the region, and Milton gambled they would, too. His best bet was to cover the primary path around the area, and getting help would increase his odds of success.

He had learned all he could here, he concluded. Best to get going. The snippets were all he'd likely get, and he couldn't follow them without them knowing. It was already late morning; he needed to use his time wisely and get a head start to reach the tavern. The action was going to be somewhere in the Black Hills region, of that, he was convinced.

An hour or so later, Milton entered the tavern, the smell of stale beer assaulting his nostrils. He glanced around, but there was no sign of Chicken's lanky frame. Approaching the bar, he ordered a beer, the wood tacky under his fingers. "Seen Chicken around, Bert?" he asked, taking a swig of the bitter brew.

The bartender grunted, wiping a mug. "He was in earlier."

Milton let out a frustrated breath. "Any idea where he went?"

"Who knows... you know him, comes and goes. Probably hanging round town like always."

Chicken, the town's fixture, was frustratingly elusive at times. Milton never knew where the man lived. Usually, he could find him at the tavern or hanging around town—or failing that, could leave a message with the bartender. But he had failed to show the last time he left a message. He needed him now. Leaving another message was no guarantee.

The tavern was relatively empty, but it was approaching noon, and it would soon be bustling. As the afternoon wore on, things got busier, but he had been unsuccessful in soliciting interest in his endeavor.

As he sat at the tavern, nursing his drink and pondering his next move, Milton's attention snapped to the entrance as the four men who had abandoned the search in the mountains shuffled into the establishment. He scrutinized them closely, noting the weariness etched into their faces and the slump in their shoulders.

The weary travelers trudged into the dimly lit tavern, their conversation filling the air and drawing Milton's attention like a moth to flame.

"...and I tell you, I've had enough of this nonsense," grumbled one of the men, his voice heavy with frustration.

"Nine days we've been chasing shadows, and for what? That runaway is long gone, mark my words."

Another chimed in, his tone equally disheartened. "Aye, and Olu's no better. Leading us on a wild goose chase through these blasted mountains. If I ever see that man again, I'll give him a piece of my mind."

Milton's ears perked up at the mention of Olu's name, his heart pounding with anticipation. Gathering his courage, he approached them, his voice tinged with urgency. "Gentlemen, may I have a word?" he asked, gesturing a request to join them at their nearby table.

They ignored his gesture, leaving him standing awkwardly."

"Excuse me, gentlemen," Milton began, his tone eager. "I couldn't help but overhear your conversation. Did I hear you mention the runaway, the one called Silas?"

The men exchanged wary glances, their expressions guarded. "Aye, what of it?" one of them replied, his tone curt.

Milton blurted out his spiel, his words pouring forth in a frantic torrent as he outlined his theory. He spoke of hidden trails and secret hideouts, of rumors and whispers that suggested Silas might still be within reach.

The men exchanged skeptical glances, clearly unconvinced by Milton's words. "Nine days we've been at this, mate," one of them grumbled. "It's a lost cause. That slave is long gone."

Milton persisted, his voice rising with desperation. "But you don't understand," he insisted. "Just today, I overheard people planning his escape. I came here to get help. This is our best, possibly the only, chance to catch those who are helping him. We can wrap this up in one or two days at most."

This one is cuckoo," one of the men commented, annoyed. They exchanged incredulous looks, their patience wearing thin. And then, without warning, the older man stood and pushed Milton aside with a forceful shove, sending him stumbling into a nearby table. "Didn't you hear? We're not interested in your wild stories. We've been hearing other people's fantasies for the past two days. Bugger off!"

Chairs clattered to the floor, tables wobbled precariously, and for a moment, the tavern was consumed by chaos. But as quickly as it had begun, the commotion subsided, and the men returned to their drinks, their resolve unshaken by Milton's interruption.

Defeated but undeterred, Milton dusted himself off and retreated to a safe distance, nursing his wounded pride as he watched the men finish their drinks and prepare to leave.

Finishing their drinks, they got up and made their way to the door, but one of the younger members of the group held back. "You guys go on; it's been a long ride, and I'm in no hurry to get back on a saddle. I'm getting another."

They said their farewells and left.

The lone man ordered another beer and sat there silently drinking, lost in his thoughts. "Hey," he said, addressing Milton.

Milton looked up, flinching as he realized he was being called, a tinge of apprehension gripping him. He had faced rejection moments ago, and the prospect of another humiliating encounter made his heart pound with unease.

"So, what makes you think Silas is still here?" he asked, his tone tinged with curious skepticism.

Milton seized the opportunity, launching into his pitch once more as he desperately tried to convince the man of the urgency of their situation. And to his relief, the man listened, albeit reluctantly, nodding in reluctant agreement as Milton's words sank in. Perhaps, he thought, there was still hope yet.

"So how much is the pay?" the man asked.

Milton faltered, not expecting the question. "I..., I," he stammered, "I know I can't offer you much in terms of payment, but I do know Mr. Thomas. He's a man of means, and if we succeed in capturing Silas, he'll see that you're duly rewarded. Trust me on this."

The man's expression softened, his curiosity piqued by the promise of potential reward. "One or two days, that's all I can spare," he muttered, casting Milton a calculating glance.

Milton nodded eagerly, relief flooding through him. "That's all I ask," he replied, gratitude evident in his voice. "With your help, we can finally put an end to this madness and bring the runaway to justice. Thank you."

As the man nodded in agreement, Milton couldn't help but feel a glimmer of hope. Perhaps his luck was finally beginning to turn.

Just then Chicken walked in. Things were definitely

improving, now he had another person.

. . .

As the day drew to a close, Thomas rode the ridgeline alongside Olu, their exhaustion evident in the weariness etched upon their faces. Suddenly, a lone rider bolted onto the ridge, his expression one of extreme excitement. "We've found him!" he exclaimed, his voice echoing across the rugged terrain.

Thomas's heart raced at the news. Finally, they had found Silas. Thoughts of what he would do with Silas when they returned to the plantation filled his mind. He would make him regret ever defying him, especially in public the way he did.

But Olu's apprehension ran deeper. He feared for Taro's safety. He had hoped to be present when they found Taro, to control the situation. These men had been frustrated for days, and there was no telling what they might have done to him in their anger.

Their concerns, though opposite, added urgency to their movements for different reasons. Spurring their horses forward, Olu and Thomas led the group to where Taro was being held captive. Each step weighed heavily on their minds. For Thomas, it was the fate of their search, and for Olu, it was Taro's well-being; both hung in the balance.

As they descended the steep mountain slopes, navigating the narrow path the rider's horse had made, a sense of tension hung heavy in the air. The urgency of the situation spurred them forward until they reached a small clearing. Four men stood there, their excitement palpable as they turned at the sound of the incoming riders.

Spud, riding behind the man who had fetched them, led the way, followed closely by Thomas and Olu. The others trailed behind Olu, their anticipation evident in their hurried movements.

As they drew closer, Olu's eyes scanned the clearing, and his heart sank at the sight of a still body lying on the ground. The men clustered around the figure, obstructing his view. Dread gripped him as he feared the worst, his mind racing with all the possible outcomes.

Pushing through the crowd, Olu finally got a clear view of the scene. He felt relief upon seeing Taro, trussed but unharmed, lying on the ground. His heart skipped a beat, and a wave of gratitude flooded through him. The boy was safe; his worst fears had not come to pass.

With a mixture of relief and concern, Olu moved closer to Taro, eager to ensure his well-being and determine what had transpired in their absence. As he knelt beside him, he breathed a silent prayer of thanks for their fortunate outcome amidst the chaos and uncertainty of their search.

Turning to Thomas, Spud announced, "I think we found your man. The clues we've found only point to one person; this must be him."

Thomas wasted no time and swiftly dismounted, his expression a mix of determination and anticipation. As he approached the bound figure, a surge of excitement coursed through him. Finally, after days of relentless pursuit, they had found their man. Pushing beside Olu, he approached the still form on the ground, his eyes narrowing as he took in the sight of the figure trussed up but unharmed.

He shifted position, avoiding touching the still body as he studied the face of the captive. He ached to see the fear in Silas's eyes when he recognized that he had found him. Instead, a flicker of resignation crossed Thomas's features as the truth dawned upon him—it wasn't Silas, it was just a boy. Thomas was engulfed by a wave of disappointment, swiftly followed by a rising tide of fury. Nine days wasted, and still no sign of his elusive prey in sight.

Doubt slowly began to gnaw at the edges of his resolve as he surveyed the scene. Silas could be anywhere by now, perhaps even in another parish. It had been too long since the escape, and the trail was now cold. As his gaze lingered on the bound boy, Thomas began to accept the harsh reality of their situation.

Frustration smoldered within him as he turned his attention to the bound boy. "Who are you?" he demanded, his voice laced with a mixture of anger and the onset of defeat. The hunt for Silas had taken its toll, but Thomas hoped maybe this boy knew something useful, some small scrap of information to keep the fire of hope burning.

Taro was scared, his eyes wide, as he turned to face the gathered men, they were all white, except for one. Why are they doing this? He had done nothing wrong, he thought.

Olu spoke then, "Are you okay, son?"

The boy did not answer, but his eyes showed a spark of relief and gratitude at the friendly voice.

"Answer him. You're safe, you've done nothing wrong. Just tell the truth. What are you doing here?"

Looking at Olu, Taro told him his reason; he was sent as punishment for something he did several days ago. He is meant to return in two days.

Thomas watched the exchange between the boy and Olu with silent detachment. He no longer felt the investment he once did. The boy's words offered nothing of value, no new hope. Too much time had passed, the trail now cold. Resigned to the reality before him, Thomas acknowledged the futility of his quest. It was time to abandon the chase and redirect his efforts elsewhere.

But there was one loose end, one last fleeting hope. He glanced at Olu, his thoughts drifting to Milton's missed deadline. Olu's forthrightness and the manner in which he had conducted the search had reinforced his initial read of the man. Milton's information, on the other hand, appeared to be baseless. He had given the man some slack to see if it would develop into something. Was it worth pursuing now? Maybe it would be foolish not to follow it to its conclusion. With any luck, he might find a fish on the line... but he wasn't convinced.

He had invested so much time already, and for what? He would give it more thought when he returned home.

25

THE HISS OF THE WIND

The sun dipped low on the horizon, casting long shadows across the rugged landscape as Milton and his gang fanned out along the forest trail. With each step, the tension in the air grew thicker, a palpable sense of anticipation mingling with the fading light of dusk. Milton's voice was firm and commanding, as he reminded his men of the rules of engagement: "If in doubt, shoot," he instructed, his words leaving no room for hesitation. The men exchanged uncertain glances, silently grappling with the weight of Milton's directive. By his calculation, no one would care about a runaway and his helpers being shot while trying to escape.

They had settled on a plan for monitoring the stretch of the trail that edged the Black Hills, a stretch Milton thought to be the more likely route the conspirators would take. Milton stationed himself to the southeast, at a point just north of where the trail turned and ran along the sea towards Hope Bay. He chose this spot for its strategic vantage point, where he could survey a long stretch in either direction. It was a lonely vigil, but one he knew was necessary if they were to have any chance of intercepting their elusive quarry.

To the northwest, Marty crouched low among the underbrush, his fingers tightening around the stock of his rifle as he peered into the gathering gloom. His task was to keep a watchful eye on the trail as it wound its way southeast through the dense forest.

In between them, hidden from view, Chicken lay in wait at his concealed vantage point, perched high atop a rocky outcrop overlooking the trail. His senses were attuned to the slightest sound or movement, his eyes scanning the shadows with unwavering focus. It was a precarious position, but one that offered the best chance of spotting their target before it was too late.

As the darkness deepened and the forest settled into an eerie stillness, Milton and his companions settled in for a long vigil. It was a waiting game now, their senses honed to razor-sharp focus as they kept watch over the shadowed expanse of the forest.

For Milton, the hours seemed to drag on endlessly, but in his core, he knew somewhere out there, Silas and his companions were moving ever closer. He prayed a silent prayer that their path would lead to him.

. . .

In the depths of the cave, Silas sat huddled with Kai and Willow, their faces illuminated by the flickering flames of small torches. The damp walls seemed to close in around them, amplifying the eerie silence that enveloped the underground chamber. Silas winced as he shifted his weight, the dull ache of his injured leg a constant reminder of their precarious situation.

Willow, her brow furrowed with concern, carefully tended to Silas's wound, her gentle touch a soothing balm against the pain. Despite the dimness of their surroundings, her steady hands worked with practiced precision, applying poultices and bandages with a sense of urgency born of desperation.

Kai, his gaze fixed on the tunnel ahead, listened intently for any sign of movement beyond the cave's confines. They had finally reached the upper cavern after a grueling journey through the connecting tunnel. For Silas, the passage was a test of endurance, his injuries hindering every movement. With Willow and Kai's support, they positioned themselves strategically to help Silas boost himself up into the upper tunnel. Using their hands and shoulders as leverage points, they assisted Silas in hoisting himself upward, inch by painful inch. Each movement was met with grim determination, Silas gritting his teeth against the pain. When he finally reached the upper cavern, his body trembled with exhaustion, but his spirit remained unbroken.

As Willow finished dressing Silas's wound, she cast a worried glance towards the mouth of the tunnel. "We need to move quickly," she whispered, her voice barely audible above the echoing whispers of the cave. "The longer we stay here, the greater the risk of discovery when we get to the trail. We need to leave the cave while there is still some darkness."

Silas nodded, his jaw set in a determined line. Despite the pain that throbbed through his injured leg, he knew they couldn't afford to delay their escape any longer. With a silent gesture to his companions, he rose to his feet, the torch held aloft to guide their way through the darkness.

Together, they moved with cautious steps towards the tunnel's entrance, the soft shuffle of their footsteps echoing off the cavern walls. As they drew closer to the mouth of the tunnel, the faint rustling of wings filled the air, sending a shiver down Silas's spine.

"Bats," he muttered, his voice tinged with unease. "They're a bad omen."

Willow squeezed his hand reassuringly, her touch a grounding presence in the midst of his fear. "We'll be fine," she said, her voice steady despite the tremor of apprehension that lingered in the air. "Just stay close, and follow my lead."

With a shared nod of determination, they stepped into the tunnel, the flickering light of the torch casting elongated shadows on the rocky walls. Ahead lay their path to freedom, a treacherous journey fraught with danger and uncertainty. But they were determined to press forward. They would deal with whatever challenges lay ahead.

· · ·

As the hours crept closer to dawn, Milton's gang found themselves battling the overwhelming urge to succumb to sleep. The darkness of the night seemed to weigh heavily upon them, pressing down with a relentless force that threatened to engulf their weary minds.

Marty, stationed at the northernmost lookout point, stifled a yawn as he scanned the horizon for any sign of movement. Nearby, Chicken lay in wait at his concealed vantage point, his senses alert for any hint of danger.

And at the southernmost point, Milton stood vigilant, his gaze fixed on the distant shadows that danced along the trail. His bad leg throbbed with a dull ache, a constant reminder of the physical toll that their pursuit had taken on his battered body.

Together, they waited in silence, each moment stretching into eternity as they grappled with the relentless march of time. But as the night wore on, the urge to sleep grew ever stronger, threatening to overwhelm their resolve. With every passing moment, they fought to stay awake, knowing that their vigilance was the only thing standing between them and the elusive target that remained just beyond their grasp.

. . .

As they walked the dimly lit tunnel, Willow's dream where she is trapped in a ravine with Kai, Silas and Kai's uncle, kept replaying in her mind. The parallels of their current situation and the dream felt ominous. In the dream, they were in a similar tunnel, running away from an unknown danger. But the part that kept playing over and over again was when they exited the tunnel... there was a flash of slithering scales vanishing into the bushes, accompanied by a hissing sound that seemed to float in the wind.

"Wait," ...she said. "Let's stop a minute," her tone trembling with apprehension. "I need to tell you something..."

They paused, exchanging uneasy glances in the dimly lit tunnel, the distant echo of dripping water creating a haunting rhythm in the silence, as they waited in anticipation for Willow to share her thoughts.

"I don't know what it means but I think I should tell you. The dream I had keeps playing in my mind..."

Kai understood what she meant, but he could see the confusion on Silas's face.

Willow recounted her dream for Silas, her voice trembling slightly as she finished. "The slithering scales disappearing into the bushes, the hissing in the wind... it keeps playing in my mind. It feels so real, like a warning. I just can't shake the feeling that danger is waiting outside."

Kai's forehead creased in concern, his eyes flickering between Willow and the direction of the tunnel's exit. "What kind of danger?" he asked, realizing the moment he said it, how futile the question must feel to them, given all the dangers facing them.

Her frustration was evident in her terse response. "I don't know, Kai..." she said, immediately regretting her tone. "I'm sorry, I didn't mean to be short. But whatever it is, it feels... real, and ominous."

Silas broke the heavy silence, voicing the obvious. But in that moment, his words held a clarity that they sought. "We already know there are dangers. In fact, there is nothing but danger in everything we have done since I ran away. Nothing's changed. It's just a reminder that we need to be extra vigilant, and be prepared for anything or everything."

The simplicity of his statement resonated within her. For Silas, it was no more dangerous to proceed than it was to not proceed, and, as far as Kai and she were concerned, they were tied to his destiny.

Kai, clearly feeling the same, nodded in agreement. "Nicely said, Silas. Then, we proceed. We must be prepared for anything," he said.

26

VANISHED

As the darkness of the night slowly began to recede, Chicken's keen eyes scanned the surrounding forest with unwavering focus. He had chosen his vantage point carefully, perched high above the trail on a rocky outcrop that offered an unobstructed view of the path below.

With every passing moment, the anticipation of spotting their elusive quarry mounted, driving him to maintain a vigilant watch. The weight of Milton's instructions lingered in the back of his mind, a constant reminder of the consequences of failure.

Below, the forest remained cloaked in shadow, its depths shrouded in mystery. The faint rustle of leaves and the distant cry of a nocturnal creature echoed through the stillness. It was a haunting melody that seemed to dance on the edge of perception.

The roof of the tunnel began closing on them as Willow, Silas and Kai approached the end of the tunnel. Silas involuntarily let out quiet groans as they dropped to their hands and knees to negotiate the low exit. The dense undergrowth surrounding the exit obscured their path, with thick bushes, brambles, and vines entwined in a chaotic tangle. Their hearts raced as they hugged the ground and crawled through the low-hanging bushes. Willow and Kai had already done this when they first found the exit, their passage then had cleared the thicker sections, making it less difficult now for Silas to negotiate.

The gash in his leg throbbed with renewed intensity and pain, as he maneuvered through the dense undergrowth. The crude bandage was beginning to stain with fresh blood, becoming damper by the reopening edges of the wound. He knew the careful healing of the past few days was being undone with each agonizing inch. Each snag of a branch, each scrape against rough bark, sent a jolt of fiery pain through his injured limb. The undergrowth seemed to close in around him like a relentless barrier, but through the branches, he finally glimpsed their goal and the promise of escape. Each painful movement brought him closer, fueling his determination with a mixture of fear and defiance.

Emerging into the dim light of dawn, they stood and cautiously made their way through the dense foliage, the faint rustling of leaves accompanying their every step. The trail beckoned from a short distance ahead, a well-used path winding through the forest under the watchful gaze of towering trees.

Pausing at the edge of the trail, Willow, Kai, and Silas exchanged cautious glances, their senses on high alert. A shiver ran down Willow's spine at the hoot of a Patoo. They listened intently, the only sounds the rustle of leaves in the gentle breeze and the distant murmur of a waterfall.

With a silent nod of understanding, they split up, each taking a different path to join the trail at separate points. Willow was the first to join the trail, her heart pounding, her eyes straining for any hint of danger. She moved with deliberate steps, the forest canopy casting shifting patterns of light and shadow as she advanced.

Kai and Silas followed suit, their movements careful and deliberate as they emerged onto the trail at different intervals. Their plan was simple yet essential—to avoid drawing attention to themselves by joining the trail as a group. As they stepped onto the path, their senses remained on edge, acutely aware of the potential dangers that lurked in the shadows.

As the first light of dawn painted the sky in hues of pink and gold, Chicken's heart quickened with anticipation. The time for action was drawing near, and he knew that every second counted in their pursuit.

With a silent prayer for success, he focused his attention once more on the trail below, his senses attuned to the slightest movement or sound. The journey ahead was fraught with danger and uncertainty, but he was determined to see it through to the end.

Suddenly, a movement caught his eye. Three figures emerged from the shadows, making their way along the forest trail. Though he had not seen them before, one of them was unmistakable to Chicken. It was the kid Milton had hired him to follow, the one he had tracked to Nanny's house just a few days ago.

His pulse quickened with excitement as he watched their progress, his mind racing with possibilities. This was it—the moment they had been waiting for.

As Chicken hurriedly descended from his rocky perch, his eyes darted back to the trail below, searching for any sign of Willow, Kai, and Silas. Moments of visibility between the dense foliage allowed him brief glimpses of their progress as they made their way along the path. However, as he stealthily maneuvered through the underbrush to rejoin the trail, he lost sight of them.

Silas and his companions moved closer to their goal, a massive Ceiba tree, unaware that they had been seen. Drawing closer to their destination, they veered off the trail into the woods, guided by the towering presence of the massive Ceiba tree. Its gnarled branches reached toward the sky like outstretched hands in worship, the faint glow of early morning casting a gentle illumination over the forest floor below.

Their objective was beyond the tree, a distant waterfall faintly reflecting the morning light. They were relieved to be off the main trail, as they set off on the path Willow and Kai had previously traveled.

Chicken was in a quandary. He had lost them. The last place he spotted them was just as they approached a towering Ceiba tree, its massive roots anchoring it firmly in the earth. He cautiously approached the towering tree, its roots spread wide and gnarled, creating natural alcoves and hiding spots under the thick foliage. With each step, he scanned the area around the massive roots, his heart pounding in his chest, careful not to make a sound.

The dim light filtering through the canopy above painted shifting patterns of shadow and dull gray light across the forest floor, shrouding the surroundings in a veil of mystery and uncertainty. As he approached the base of the tree, he slowed his pace, his eyes scanning from shadow to shadow in search of any signs of movement. The roots of the massive tree loomed large and imposing, their twisted forms creating a labyrinth of hiding places. It was possible they had stopped among the roots to catch their breath or assess their surroundings.

With each passing moment, a knot of tension tightened further in Chicken's stomach. He knew he had to find them, but the vastness of the forest and the uncertainty of their whereabouts pressed down upon him. Clenching his fist, he scanned the area frantically, the pulse in his temple throbbing with frustration.

They couldn't have disappeared so quickly, especially not on such a straight stretch of trail; it was a clear shot for about a quarter mile before it bent out of sight. Even if they had run, he would have surely heard their footsteps echoing through the quiet forest. His mind raced with possibilities, but none of them provided any comfort.

Suddenly, movement beyond the Ceiba tree, off the trail, caught his eye. Was it an animal? Or perhaps it was them, trying to avoid detection? With bated breath, Chicken edged closer, his senses on high alert as he prepared to investigate. Then, he saw them about a hundred yards ahead, heading in the direction of a waterfall. Overwhelmed with relief, a growing confidence steered him as he followed in the shadows. The trees and bushes were the perfect cover.

As they approached the falls, the roar of cascading water grew louder, mingling with the symphony of the forest. Chicken started closing the distance between them, relying on the heavy foliage and the deafening torrent of water to mask his approach. However, he lost sight of them as they made a turn towards a wall-like structure beside the falls; a steep imposing section of the mountainside. A patch of dense foliage blocking his view.

The roar of the water became deafening as the trio

approached the mountain wall; a sheer expanse of moss-covered rock slick with spray from the falls. There, they made a brief stop for Willow to tend to Silas's wounds, now open from the stress of the journey. He winced as she bound it tightly, then they were ready to go.

The deafening cascade of water drowned out all other sounds, forcing them to communicate with urgent gestures and pointed glances as they executed the plan laid out during their earlier scouting mission. Willow pointed confidently toward a series of boulders, a path she and Kai had determined offered the safest passage, considering Silas's injury. Despite the throbbing pain, Silas was now driven by adrenaline. They were so close.

With Kai's help, Silas maneuvered over the slippery rocks, his labored breaths a sharp counterpoint to the thunderous roar of the falls. The pull of the waterfall was relentless, a constant threat to sweep them off their feet—a danger they knew lay in wait beyond the ledge.

Step by painful step, they navigated the treacherous path, one rock after another, until they reached the edge of the cascade. Willow looked at Silas, gesturing to where he should grab hold as she placed her hand through the thundering veil of water. Once she was confident he understood, she took a steadying breath and plunged into the deafening torrent, her figure disappearing instantly.

Kai turned to Silas, silently offering assistance. Grimacing, Silas braced himself and followed Willow into the roaring cascade. For a heart-stopping moment, he was blinded and buffeted by the force of the water, but then Kai's strong grasp steadied him as Willow grabbed his other arm, helping him through. Finally, Kai followed suit, navigating the deafening torrent with determination.

Finally, they reached their destination—a narrow ledge hidden behind the wall of water. Soaked and shivering, they huddled together for a brief respite, the roaring water muffling any sounds of potential pursuit. For now, they were safe, a sliver of hope ignited against the odds. Kai took the lead, pointing to a hole in the mountain wall. It was their passage to Silas's rebirth.

As Chicken cautiously approached the area where he had

last seen his quarry, a sense of unease gnawed at him. He was well aware of the high risks of being discovered and the dire consequences that could follow. Taking a moment to steady his nerves, he waited in the shadows, straining his ears for any sign of movement. Had they hidden on the other side of the dense foliage? Or had they moved on? Despite the deafening roar, a hawk's mournful wailing cry pierced the air as it flew by.

After an agonizing wait, he judged it safe to proceed. With slow and deliberate steps, he advanced, his senses on high alert. The forest seemed to hold its breath around him, as if anticipating his next move. He couldn't shake the feeling that they were just around the bend, watching his every move.

As he rounded the corner, dread settled like a heavy weight in the pit of his stomach. They were nowhere in sight. His first instinct was to assume they had continued towards the falls. However, he knew that the area around the falls offered little foliage cover, making it risky for him to approach without being seen.

Pausing to reassess the situation, he decided on doubling back a bit, searching for an alternate route that would afford him some cover as he made his way towards the falls. Every second mattered, but he couldn't afford to rush into a potentially dangerous situation.

When he finally reached his intended vantage point, offering a full view of the edge of the falls and the open area around it, it became clear they weren't anywhere in sight. He was overwhelmed with frustration and fear as he grappled with the implications of their disappearance.

His mind raced with questions. Had they somehow detected his presence and fled? Or had they simply continued on their journey, oblivious to his pursuit? The uncertainty gnawed at him, filling him with a sense of helplessness as he contemplated his next move.

Despite his mounting anxiety, Chicken knew he couldn't afford to give up. He had come too far to let them slip through his fingers now. With a steely resolve, he pushed aside his doubts and focused on the task at hand. He would find them, no matter what it took.

27

REBIRTH

The deafening, reverberating roar behind the falls made communication nearly impossible. Their clothes clung uncomfortably to their bodies, soaked through by the relentless cascade, while swirling mist obscured their surroundings. Shivers racked their bodies, teeth chattering uncontrollably as Kai gestured towards the narrow opening in the rock face, barely visible through the mist. It marked the entrance to their next challenge: a steep and treacherous ascent into the heart of the mountain.

Silas, his nerves already frayed, couldn't help but feel a sense of apprehension as they prepared to embark on this new leg of their journey. The sight of the narrow passage ahead, coupled with the first glimpses of bats flitting through the dim light, sent a shiver down his spine. He drew closer to Willow and Kai, seeking solace in their presence amidst the eerie surroundings.

With a silent nod of understanding, they began their ascent, their footsteps echoing against the cavern walls as they ventured deeper into the narrow passage. The presence of bats became more pronounced with each passing moment, their dark shadows dancing against the rock as they flitted overhead. Silas couldn't suppress a shudder at the sight, his unease palpable in the tense set of his shoulders.

"Are you alright, Silas?" Willow's voice cut through the

darkness, filled with concern.

Silas nodded, though the tension in his muscles betrayed his inner turmoil. "Just not a fan of bats," he admitted, his voice barely above a whisper. "They give me the creeps."

Kai offered a reassuring smile. "Don't worry, Silas. They're not used to us being here. We'll be out of here soon."

Despite their reassurances, Silas couldn't shake the feeling of dread that gnawed at him with each passing moment.

As Kai led the way through the intricate cracks in the rock, Silas and Willow followed closely behind, their senses heightened by the oppressive darkness that surrounded them. With each step, they had to navigate carefully, mindful of the treacherous terrain that threatened to twist an ankle or trap a foot in the narrow fissures.

Suddenly, the silence was broken by a noise that sounded like movement across loose stones. Something must have been startled by their approach. The sounds reverberated through the cavern, sending shivers down their spines. They froze, hearts pounding, eyes wide with apprehension. Kai glanced around, searching for the source of the disturbance, his hand instinctively reaching for anything that might serve as a makeshift weapon. But in the darkness of the cave, there was nothing within reach.

Suddenly, just ahead, from a narrow split in the wall about a foot wide, something burst into the path—it was an animal. Willow stifled a scream, Silas's breath caught in his throat, and Kai tensed, ready to react at a moment's notice. It took them a moment to realize it was a goat. The animal, wild-eyed and panicked, darted back and forth, seeking an escape route from the confines of the cave.

Their presence blocked its only path to freedom, turning the animal's fear into desperation as it realized it was trapped. Silas's own fear intensified, mirroring the animal's panic as he watched it race away, then back towards them, desperately seeking another path of escape, its hooves thundering against the rocky ground. Then, realizing there was no other exit, it stopped, locking eyes with Kai. Kai shuddered—not from fear of goats, but from the realization that its only escape was through them. He sensed desperation awakening its primal instincts: flight or fight. And they stood in the only way for flight. Only one option left.

Kai calmly whispered to Silas and Willow, "Back up slowly, don't make any sudden moves."

Willow backed up, Silas and Kai following her lead, their eyes fixed on the stressed and trapped animal. The path began to widen a bit, and Willow squeezed against the wall, telling the others to do the same as she continued to inch backward. The trapped animal sensed an opening. It was hardly wide enough, but it had to act quickly in case it closed.

The goat made a mad dash directly towards Kai, its hooves reverberating through the confined space. Kai flinched as it raced towards him, shifting at the last minute towards the narrow space. As the goat raced past them, its panicked eyes locking with theirs for a brief, heart-stopping moment, Silas felt a surge of empathy wash over him. In that instant, he understood the animal's fear, its desperate need to escape, and he shared in its vulnerability.

Then, as quickly as it had appeared, the goat was gone, disappearing into the darkness of the cavern, leaving behind a trail of echoes and the lingering scent of fear. The bats, disturbed by the commotion, took flight in a chaotic flurry, their wings brushing against their faces as they disappeared into the shadows. Silas cowered against the wall, hands instinctively covering his head, as the swarming bats awakened by the goat's frantic movements filled the air around them. His heart pounded in his chest, his breaths coming in short, shallow gasps as his fear of bats consumed him.

To Silas, bats were more than just creatures of the night; they were harbingers of doom, symbols of impending misfortune. His superstitions ran deep, ingrained in him from childhood tales of darkness and danger.

As the bats swooped and circled overhead, their eerie screeches and the sound of fluttering wings reverberated off the cavern walls, filling the space with a cacophony. Silas felt a chill run down his spine as he watched their erratic movements. The musty scent of guano hung heavy in the air, mixing with the damp earthiness of the cave. It was as if the very atmosphere around him had thickened with foreboding, suffocating him with its weight.

Willow and Kai, sensing Silas's distress, moved closer to

him, offering silent reassurance as they watched the frenzied bats fly away. They stayed there for a while, catching collective breaths. As they prepared to resume their trek, Willow suggested to Silas to put the blanket she had left with him in the cave over his head and shoulders. She said it may not be much, but would offer him some sense of protection from the bats.

Silas did not need any encouragement to do so. He would take any tips they had to offer, if it meant him surviving the trip through these bat-infested paths.

As they journeyed deeper into the heart of the Black Hills, little did Kai, Silas, and Willow realize they were venturing into the remnants of an ancient volcano. Once a fiery behemoth, the volcano now lay dormant, its molten fury cooled into solid rock.

Their path, hidden within the maze-like crevices of the mountain, wasn't just a trail; it was a testament to the volcano's tumultuous past. The fissures, cracks, and deep gorges that marked their route were the very channels through which rivers of molten lava once flowed, propelled by the earth's inner turmoil, before bursting into the sky in powerful eruptions that transformed the land.

They had been walking for a couple of hours, the steep incline slowly leveling off as they ventured deeper into the mountain. As they turned a corner, their path ended abruptly. A gaping gorge yawned before them, its shadowy depths stretching into an inky abyss.

As Kai, Silas, and Willow approached the gorge's edge, a colony of bats erupted from the depths, disturbed by their presence. Silas's heart pounded, breaths coming in short gasps as he struggled to control his fear.

"We can't see the bottom," Willow said, uncertainty lacing her voice. "It's too deep to descend."

Kai nodded in agreement as he scanned the rocky walls, searching for any sign of a path. Then he spotted it—a narrow ledge, barely wide enough for a single foot, protruding from the cliff face. Rocks jutted randomly from the wall, offering precarious handholds.

"That might be our only option," Willow said, following his gaze. "It looks treacherous but doable if we're careful."

"Should we cross as a group? Tie ourselves together?" Kai asked.

Silas shook his head, determination in his voice. "I have to do this alone. I can't risk you both getting hurt because of me."

Kai and Willow exchanged a worried glance. They understood Silas's need to protect them, but they couldn't shake the pang of concern for their friend.

"We understand, Silas," Kai said, regret heavy in his voice. "But..."

"Wait," Silas said, holding his ground, his resolve unwavering. "I appreciate it, but I'll see you on the other side."

He couldn't bear the thought of putting them in danger. This journey was about his rebirth. This was his test to face, his first step towards a new life.

"No," he said resolutely. "I'm doing this alone."

Kai and Willow decided to do it together, but untethered. With deep breaths, they began inching along the narrow ledge, pressing their bodies against the rocky wall. Each step was a battle against fear with the abyss looming beneath them.

Then it was Silas's turn. He approached the ledge, determination warring with panic. He knew he could do this. Slowly, he began making his way across, taking small, deliberate steps.

The air thrummed with the sound of beating wings as the bats swirled overhead, their cries amplifying his terror. Silas forced himself to focus, blocking out the fear that threatened to overwhelm him. Inch by agonizing inch, he made his way until Kai grabbed his leading arm.

Finally, they all stood on solid ground once more. Relief and wonder washed over Silas as they gazed out at the vast expanse they had conquered. They had persevered, and now they stood at the threshold of Silas's new refuge.

The narrow underground passage led to a small cavern, its walls jet-black from ancient volcanic activity. Light filtered in from a hole in the roof, about a foot above them, casting a warm glow within the chilly space. The air was heavy with the scent of earth and sea, a reminder of the forces that had shaped this sacred place.

Climbing up through the hole, onto an expansive rocky plateau, they were greeted by a sweeping view of the ocean stretching out before them, its azure waters shimmering in the sunlight. A gentle cool breeze carried the tang of the sea and the sweet scent of wildflowers. Below, fertile lands sprawled, vibrant with lush vegetation and colorful blooms. It was a breathtaking sight, a stark contrast to the forbidding barrenness they had encountered on their journey.

As they took in the beauty of their surroundings, a sense of awe washed over them. Despite the devastation wrought by fire and upheaval, life had returned to the land, reclaiming its rightful place amidst the ruins.

The once-barren terrain now teemed with life, from the whispering grasses to the towering trees that swayed gently in the ocean breeze. Birds soared overhead, their melodious songs echoing through the air, while colorful butterflies flitted among the blossoms, painting the landscape with splashes of vibrant hues.

Unknown to the travelers as they stood admiring the view, below their feet lay a hidden secret yet to be discovered. Beneath the picturesque landscape lay an intricate network of tunnels and caverns, remnants of ancient volcanic activity that had shaped the land over millennia. A perfect refuge for the hunted and persecuted.

Kai's keen observation and power of deduction brought a playful edge to their reverie as he remarked, "I bet there are more caves and tunnels scattered around here," he commented, his eyes scanning the horizon with a speculative glint. "Perfect places to disappear and hide."

He grinned mischievously at Silas, knowing full well the man's apprehension towards the dark recesses of the earth. "Looks like you'll have to overcome your fear of bats and start exploring, my friend."

Willow laughed at Kai's comment, smiling at Silas. "I think he's already begun. He did great crossing that gorge by himself, with bats hovering."

Silas chuckled nervously at Kai's teasing, understanding the underlying truth in his words. Despite his trepidation, he knew that exploring the hidden passages would be essential for his safety in this newfound refuge amidst the Black Hills.

For Silas, the sight of his newfound sanctuary stirred a torrent of emotions within him. After enduring ten days of hiding in the suffocating darkness of a cave, never daring to venture beyond its confines, the vibrant beauty and tranquility of this place felt like a revelation. It was more than just a refuge; it was hope, a freedom he had never known. As he stood on the rocky plateau, bathed in the warm glow of the sun, Silas felt a surge of ecstasy wash over him. He swore he would never again be another man's property. Here, amidst the fertile lands and hidden caverns of the Black Hills, he found a sense of safety and a chance at a new beginning, one he envisioned sharing with others in his predicament.

With a heart full of resolve, he gave thanks for Kai, Willow, and the other unknown faces that risked everything to bring him to this sacred place.

They had spent several hours exploring the hidden wonders of Silas's newfound sanctuary together, forging bonds that would last a lifetime. Now, it was late afternoon, and they needed to depart. They had a long journey back. They gathered their belongings and prepared to bid farewell.

Willow's eyes glistened with unshed tears, but she refused to let them fall. Instead, she enveloped Silas in a warm embrace, her silent promise of a future reunion evident in the lingering embrace. "We'll be back to check on you, Silas," she whispered, her voice choked with emotion.

Silas nodded, his gratitude evident in his gaze. "Thank you, both of you, for everything," he replied, his voice filled with sincerity.

As they made their way back towards the entrance of the cavern, Silas trailing behind them, they crested a rise and came face to face with Chicken.

The air crackled with tension as they locked eyes, his grip tightening on the gun in his hand.

28

THE SACRIFICE

Chicken was just as startled as they were to see them, his grip tightening on the gun in his hand as memories of Milton's directives flooded his mind. "If in doubt, shoot," Milton had instructed, leaving no room for hesitation. Chicken felt the weight of the decision pressing down on him, his unease growing with each passing second.

As he stood facing Silas and his companions, the memories of Milton's ruthless orders clashed with his own sense of uncertainty. He wished he had gone back and retrieved Milton and Marty when he had lost them behind the falls. Then it wouldn't be his decision to make. But driven by curiosity, he had ventured closer to the edge, hoping to catch a glimpse of their fate.

As Chicken navigated the treacherous terrain along the edge of the waterfalls, a sudden misstep sent him careening towards the rushing torrent below. The powerful force of the water seized him, its icy grip shocking as he was dragged under. For a terrifying moment, he was engulfed in darkness, his body battered against the jagged rocks as the tumbling water propelled him towards the bottom of the icy pool, where it held him powerless against the rocky bottom.

Miraculously, his struggle forced him out of the direct path of the tumbling torrent, subtly changing its force from a trapping weight to one that aided his escape. Once released from its grip, the plummeting torrent propelled him towards the rocky wall of the mountain. There, he managed to find a tenuous grip with his fingers, his foot scrambling futilely for purchase on the slick rock face. With bursting lungs, searing red hot from the desperate need for air, he fought against the relentless pull of the water. His world began to darken as his brain starved for oxygen, his free hand flailing for purchase.

Finally, with a final burst of effort, Chicken heaved himself upward, tearing a nail from his finger in the process. Bruised and battered from the ordeal, his injured hand gripping desperately, his outstretched hand found the edge of the flat ledge above him. With one last effort, he pulled himself up, gasping for breath. He lay there, gasping, coughing and sputtering, the waterfall's roar pounding in his ears as he desperately filled his lungs.

Now, Chicken stood face to face with Silas and his companions, his heart pounding in his chest, torn between loyalty to Milton and the nagging doubts that gnawed at his conscience. He knew he had a choice to make, one that could alter the course of their lives forever.

As the standoff between Chicken and the group unfolded, a dark shadow crept across the land, swallowing the fading sunlight as thick clouds gathered on the horizon.

At first, the wind stirred gently, barely a whisper against the rugged landscape, then it began to steadily increase, pushing the thick clouds nearer. In the distance, the sky darkened, the ominous clouds looming larger with each passing moment. Lightning flickered within their depths, a silent threat of the tempest to come. A distant rumble of thunder echoed through the air, its low growl growing steadily louder as the storm approached.

The winds turned into urgent gusts that tugged at clothing and flattened the tall grass covering the area.

Silas and his companions exchanged wary glances, their senses on high alert as the tension in the air mounted. With the storm on the horizon, they knew they had little time to seek shelter before its fury was unleashed upon them.

Chicken, acutely aware of the need to find shelter, had to make a decision. As darkness descended rapidly, transitioning from sunshine to dusk, the rain began to fall, driven by violent gusts of wind. He hesitated, unsure whether to fire at Silas, when suddenly the air around him detonated with the force of a cannon, his ears ringing, a blinding flash of white-hot fire following as lightning struck a tree behind Chicken.

Silas caught glimpses of the chaotic scene as he and the others dove to the ground for safety. He saw the lightning strike the tree behind Chicken—a blinding flash of white-hot energy that illuminated the darkened landscape, briefly etching jagged lines across the sky. The crackling bolt ignited the tree, sending sparks flying and billowing smoke into the air. The acrid smell of smoke mingled with the earthy scent of the rain. Startled by the sudden burst of light and deafening roar, Chicken instinctively ducked. While simultaneously turning around to see what had caused the massive explosion behind him, he lost his footing and his balance. Silas saw the look of alarm on his face just before he vanished from sight, disappearing into the gaping hole.

Then, as quickly as it had begun, the storm began to recede, the clouds parting to allow the sun to once again bathe the land in its warm light.

The sudden change in the weather left Willow feeling unsettled, her thoughts drifting to Aiyanna's words about the legend: "Anyone who ventures there with evil in their heart is immediately consumed by fire." Despite trying to dismiss it as mere fantasy, her upbringing under Nanny's guidance left her unable to completely shake off the feeling of foreboding. She couldn't ignore the nagging sense that there might be truth to the old tales, especially considering her own dreams and Nanny's revelation of her newfound Gift of Sight. Something she had yet to come to terms with.

As they rose from the place they sought refuge during the storm, Willow's mind raced with apprehension. The echoes of the legend, which cast a shadow over their surroundings, intensified her unease. It was in this moment of uncertainty that Kai's voice broke through her thoughts, his tone urgent and filled with concern.

"He fell into the hole," Kai began, his voice tinged with worry. "I saw something when the storm hit. The man... he fell into the hole."

Shaken, Silas nodded. "I saw it too."

Willow's heart skipped a beat at their words, her fear for Chicken's safety amplifying the unease that gripped her. She exchanged a worried glance with Silas, their shared concern mirrored in their expressions."

Uncertain of whether Chicken still possessed the gun, they hesitated before deciding to rush to his aid. They cautiously approached, spotting the fallen gun on the ground a short distance from the hole. Relieved, they hurried to the hole, but it was quickly replaced by concern as they saw Chicken lying injured on the floor of the hole.

It was evident that Chicken had sustained serious injuries, possibly even broken ribs from his fall onto a rock. His eyes wide with panic, he recoiled when he saw them, his breath coming in ragged gasps as he clutched his injured side.

"Don't move," Kai urged, his voice firm yet reassuring, "we'll help you." But despite Kai's earnest attempt to offer assistance, Chicken's fear seemed to overwhelm any rational thought.

Willow's voice, soft and reassuring, pleaded with him to stay put, promising that they meant no harm and only wanted to help him. But Chicken seemed unable to hear her words over the pounding of his own heartbeat, his mind consumed by the visceral instinct to flee

With a pained grimace, Chicken staggered backward, his movements awkward and unsteady as he hobbled away into the darkness of the passage.

"Wait! We will help you!" Kai called out desperately, his voice echoing off the cave walls.

But Chicken was gone, they could hear his frantic movements carrying him deeper into the passages of the cave. Willow exchanged a worried glance with Kai, their silent communication conveying their shared concern for Chicken's well-being.

Then, as if in response to the escalating tension, a piercing scream shattered the stillness of the cave, echoing off the rocky walls with chilling intensity. Willow's heart clenched at the sound, her mind racing with fear for Chicken's safety.

Moments later, a rush of wings filled the air as bats swarmed out of the hole, their frantic flight a stark reminder of the chaos that had unfolded in their midst.

"What have we done?" Willow gasped, looking at Kai.

"We did not do anything," Silas replied, his voice tinged with concern, "it's not our fault."

Kai, feeling a sense of responsibility, decided he needed to investigate further. Without hesitation, he descended into the cavern, disappearing into the darkness below.

Anxious moments passed before Kai returned, his expression grim.

"I think it's what we feared," he said solemnly, his voice echoing in the cavern. "In his panic, he must have forgotten the gorge and fallen in."

They stayed there for a while, not knowing what they should do. Kai and Willow were reluctant to leave in the wake of the unsettling incident. Silas, recognizing their uncertainty, stepped forward with a sense of determination. "Go," he said firmly, his voice carrying an undertone of assurance. "I'll handle things here." With a gentle yet firm encouragement, he reminded them of the journey that still lay ahead, urging them to continue despite the unsettling incident. With solemn nods and heartfelt promises exchanged, Willow and Kai entered the cavern, their footsteps echoing softly as they turned to leave Silas behind.

Silas mused to himself. "So this is what freedom feels like," he thought. He looked up at the sky, now clear and serene, amazed at how quickly it had changed. It was as if the elements themselves had conspired to save him. His gaze then shifted to the tree, its charred trunk standing as a solemn testament to the violent forces of nature. It was the sacrifice that provided him his chance at survival. Silas felt a profound sense of gratitude well up within him, realizing the magnitude of the gift he had been given.

"...Hold fast, Silas, the stars shine brightest when the night is darkest. Hold fast when hope appears lost. Find strength in that. Let it light your path."

His mother's words played through his mind as he looked out across the ocean. She was right; he had found strength in hope, and its light had led him here, to his refuge and the place of his rebirth.

ABOUT THE BOOK AND ITS AUTHOR

I have always been fascinated by Jamaica's rich history; such a small island with such a remarkable influence on the world. Today, it's renowned for its natural beauty and the island's enduring legacy in music and sports, but its impact reaches as far back as the 17th and 18th centuries.

Back then, sugar was one of the world's greatest wealth-producing industries, with Jamaica being Britain's largest producer in the Caribbean. The need for efficiency in sugar production spurred technological advancements, positioning the island as one of the early catalysts of the Industrial Revolution. The resulting wealth fueled further innovation, modernizing British cities like Liverpool and Bristol. It also created new industries and diversifying others such as banking and insurance.

Yet, behind the stories of success lies a mostly forgotten tale —that of the island's original inhabitants, the Tainos, and the Africans who were transported there. This immense wealth generated by sugar, was tragically built on the backs of enslaved Africans and came at the price of decimating the island's indigenous Taino inhabitants; a process that began with the arrival of the Spanish and continued under the British.

As a child, growing up in Jamaica, I was taught that the Tainos had all died under the harsh conditions imposed by the Spanish. However, current history and modern evidence, such as DNA research, reveal the presence of indigenous Taino ancestry amongst the Accompong Town Maroons, suggesting some mixing and possible survival. Moore Town Maroons, also known as Nanny Town, in particular, preserve a strong claim to Taino heritage.

The notion that Tainos may have coexisted with the Windward Maroons in the rugged terrain of the Blue

Mountains intrigues me. It opens up a realm of new questions and exciting possibilities: What was life like for those who survived? How did they navigate a peace treaty heavily favoring the British, and what were their experiences during that tumultuous period?

The Secret Pact, set in the Blue Mountains of Jamaica in 1743, three years after the end of the First Maroon War, imagines just that through the lives of characters like Willow and Kai, along with their band of unlikely conspirators.

The story unfolds amidst historical figures such as Nanny, one of Jamaica's enigmatic national heroes, Quao, Jeddo, and Lt. Thickenesse, whose memoirs provide invaluable insight into the era. His writings are one of the few—if not the only—sources that offer a description of Nanny, who is described in legends as a practitioner of Obeah.

This fictional tale transports readers into the past, blending historical events and places with imagined characters and narratives. It offers readers a glimpse into the past through the imagined lives intertwined with the setting and legacy of the Windward Maroons' resistance.

For additional details on the book and the themes and events mentioned in the book that are based on actual history, visit:

https://fiwiroots.com/secretpact/